Enter the Jackal

By Jonathan W. Sweet

A BRICK PICKLE PULP

Also by Jonathan W. Sweet

Nonfiction
DeForest: A Small-Town Wisconsin History
The Beginner's Guide to Pulp Fiction, Vol. 1
The Beginner's Guide to Pulp Fiction, Vol. 2
Minnesota's 50 Greatest Baseball Players
Minnesota's Great Authors

Fiction
Red Jackal Mysteries
Ghosts of the Jackal
Eye of Vengeance

Lincoln's Avenger (*forthcoming*)

Collections
Chattering Rods & Private Hawkshaws
CNI: Classified, Vol. 2
Minnesota Not-So-Nice
Pulp Adventures on the Moon
Pulp from the Pyramids
Mystery Men (& Women), Vol. 9
Mystery Men (& Women), Vol. 10 (*forthcoming*)

More Brick Pickle Pulps

The Best of *Thrilling Detective*, Volumes 1 & 2

The Best of W.C. Tuttle
Volume 1: Tombstone & Speedy, Range Detectives
Volume 2: Postings from Piperock
Volume 3: Cowpunchers & Bushwhackers

The Best of Robert Leslie Bellem
Volume 1: Chattering Rods & Private Hawkshaws
Volume 2 (Forthcoming)

Chicago Pulp Tales

Deck the Pulps

Minnesota Not-So-Nice

Pulp Adventures on the Moon

Pulp from the Pyramids

Pulp with a Bite

Thrilling Detective Pulp Tales, Volumes 1-6

Table of Contents

Dead Ball

The Red Jackal takes on Death on the Diamond!

I

ALL HE'D wanted was to have a little fun. A night out before starting a new gig. Oh, God, why had he gone to the –

SLAP!

His train of thought was interrupted by the blow to his face. "He's all yours, Coop," the gorilla of a man in front of him said as he stepped out of the way.

"Now, we're going to try this again," the one they called Coop said. "Why were you at The Pines? And what were you doing listening to our little talk?"

"I didn't hear a thing," the young man blubbered. "I was just looking to relax. The bartender at the hotel told me it was a great place to get a few drinks and meet some girls. That's all I wanted! I swear!"

"Now, see, I just don't believe you. Fred?"

This time it was a punch to his stomach that doubled the man over, causing him to throw up those drinks he had so eagerly anticipated.

A look of disgust crossed Coop's face as he moved back toward the prisoner, carefully stepping to avoid the steaming pool. "One ... more ... time. I am losing my patience. WHAT ... DID ... YOU ... HEAR?"

The man flinched and struggled to catch his breath.

"OK, OK," he gasped. "I heard you, but I don't know what you were talking about. I don't know who you are. I don't know who this Sullivan is. It means nothing to me, I swear."

Coop nodded to Fred, who slipped out of the room. Coop would have been able to handle this rube even if he hadn't been tied up. He could have left this to the boys, but sometimes you just have to take care of problems yourself. A good leader knows when to delegate and when to get hands-on, he thought to himself.

He turned back to the bound man. "Now see that's much better. Relax, we're almost done here."

He leaned in toward the man, with a sinister smile that did nothing to improve his looks. It was easy to see why he was known in the underworld as, simply, Creepy.

"Just one question left: Did you tell anyone about what you heard? One of the waitresses maybe? A fellow gambler? A friendly girl at the bar?"

"No, no, nobody knows. I won't tell a soul, I swear. You've

got to believe me!"

"Oh, I believe you," Coop said, nodding again to Fred, who had returned to the small room.

"Thank you, thank you, thank you," the man repeated as he looked up, only to notice what was in Fred's hand as he stepped out of the shadows. Looking down the barrel, he only had time to start a short prayer before everything exploded, and then went black.

II
12 hours earlier

"STRIKE TWO!"

Hamm briefly turned and glared at the umpire that had called the nasty curveball a strike, before turning his attention back to the pitcher.

The southpaw on the mound wiped the sweat off his forehead, checked the runner at first and hurled a rocket of a fastball to the plate. Hamm swung but was well behind the pitch as he heard it hit the catcher's glove.

"Strike three – you're out!"

A few boos rang down from the stands as the home team went down to defeat, but not many fans had bothered to stay until the end of the 9-0 defeat. The chilly, overcast May day had kept even most of the hardy baseball fans away from Lexington Park for that day's exhibition game.

Two who had ventured out were now standing behind home plate. The men, while both bundled up, seemed a mismatched pair. One stood over six feet tall, with handsome movie-star looks that served him well on the Minneapolis social scene. The other was almost as wide as he was tall, barely topping five feet and tipping the scales well north of 200 lbs.

"What did I tell you? This boy is something special," the

shorter said, gesturing at the pitcher who was making his way in their direction.

"Heckuva game, Josh," he said, now turning his attention to the pitcher. "Twelve strikeouts, three hits. That's why you're going to be a star."

"Thank you, Mr. Moore. I been better. I always pitch better when it gets warmer."

"It'll be plenty hot before you know it. This here is Mr. Blake Randolph," he said, indicating the other man. "He's from Brickton, just west of here. He owns the paper and radio station there and is going to be one of the investors in the new team."

"I'm thinking about it, Rob," Randolph interrupted. "I'm still not sure about putting a professional baseball team up on the Iron Range. I'm not sure about investing in any new business in this economy."

"I'm not worried," Moore said. "Roosevelt's only been in office a couple of months and things are already getting better. This depression's going to be over in a year. When that happens, the resorts are going to start booming again."

Moore was the owner of the Vermilion Bay Resort on northern Minnesota's Lake Ludlow, considered one of the finest walleye lakes in the state, if not the country. He'd also been a standout catcher, even playing a couple of years of professional ball. That was what had brought the New York native to Minnesota when he played for the Virginia Ore Diggers of the state's Northern League. When the team folded in 1916, he stayed on the Iron Range.

Before the Depression, he had personally funded a rail line extension directly to his resort – an investment that almost sank his fortunes after the stock market crash. His latest idea to drive business to his lakeside resort was to host a baseball team on the grounds.

"Josh, why don't you go ahead and go? I have some more I need to talk to Mr. Randolph about. The car is waiting to take you back to the Hopkins," Moore said, referring to the hotel the pitcher was using as a temporary home. "We've got breakfast at 8 tomorrow morning with Senator Charles, so keep the rabble-rousing to a minimum."

"Yes, sir. See you tomorrow."

"Where you been hiding him?" Randolph asked after Josh moved out of earshot.

"He was playing town ball in La Seuer. His older sister is the hostess at our restaurant and told me about him when I started talking about the baseball team. I checked him out last fall and liked what I saw."

A note of desperation crept into Moore's voice.

"I need this, Blake. Everybody loves baseball. Even if it doesn't bring in the tourists, the locals will turn out. Cheap entertainment is important these days, and we don't have a lot of other options up there.

"Josh is an important part of those plans. You saw how good he is as a hitter and a pitcher. I've got him signed for this year and that's probably all I'm going to get. As soon as word gets out about this kid, someone's going to scoop him up."

Randolph hated to see anyone in trouble. Too many of his friends had been laid low by this damned Depression. He sure hoped Rob was right and Roosevelt could get things running again. It had gotten ugly out there. Luckily, the Randolph family had thus far weathered the Depression better than most. That put him in a position to help those less fortunate, and the family had donated thousands of dollars to help fill food banks and fund other relief efforts.

At the same time, it made him an obvious source of funding for anyone in trouble – a fact that was putting plenty of strain on his friendships with other businessmen. His unwillingness to help everyone that asked for it had already ended a few relationships.

Moore could sense his indecision.

"Tell you what, Blake. The rest of the team is already up at the Vermilion. I'm taking Josh on the train tomorrow afternoon – the 1:30 out of Union Depot. Come with us, check out the field, see the team. You'll be impressed. I promise."

Rob was different than those minor acquaintances who had put the touch on him. Although he was eight years Blake's senior, they had served together in France during The Great War. That bond was one that was hard to ignore and Randolph knew he would do whatever he could to get Rob through this mess.

"I'll come up, Rob, but on one condition. I'm paying my own way – besides, I don't want people to see me with such an unsavory individual as a baseball owner. You know, all that spitting and scratching and such really won't help my reputation," he said with a wide grin.

"Ha ha, very funny. But fine, why don't you meet us at Union Depot tomorrow afternoon. The 1:30, don't forget. And Blake," he said, turning serious. "Thank you. I mean it."

"Alright. Don't expect me to hug you or anything. I'll see you tomorrow."

III

AT 10 A.M. the next morning, Blake was in one of his favorite spots: looking out at the newsroom from his glass office. For years, Blake had started almost every day at the *Brickton Gazette*. Of all the Randolph family businesses, it had always been his favorite – there was something about the excitement of a newsroom that got his blood flowing. Only the family's radio station, KBGZ, could rival it. He had just settled into his office at the *Gazette* when his star reporter, Jennifer Jones, rushed in.

"Chief," she started, needling him with her usual sarcastic greeting.

He had known the 28-year-old reporter for almost her entire life as the younger sister of his best childhood friend. Blake and

Eddie Jones had signed up to fight the Kaiser together, but only Blake had returned from France. Their long history – along with her the girl-you-wished-lived-next-door looks – led some to question her abilities, but anyone who followed her reporting soon learned she deserved her role as the paper's top newshound.

"Is this about the Red Jackal?" he asked, preparing himself for their usual discussion. "Let me guess. He was spotted again last night, with Paul Bunyan and Buck Rogers?"

A dark look crossed the reporter's face – a look that Blake knew all too well.

"Laugh all you want, but the Red Jackal is real. I was talking to Willy Olson last night and he said the Red Jackal just broke up that bank robbery two nights ago at the 1st National."

"What are you doing spending time with that weasel? Olson's a degenerate gambler and a creep of the highest caliber."

"What's the matter, Chief? Jealous?" Jennifer replied with a mischievous grin.

"That has nothing to do with … Listen … well, the point is, you can't believe a thing he says." To the usually self-composed Blake's occasional frustration, only Jennifer could leave him this flustered.

Jennifer's smile broadened as she continued, "He's not the only one. You know that. The rumors are everywhere. When are you going to let me write about this? Every criminal in Brickton is talking about him."

As a journalist, Blake was aware he was walking a fine line. He'd never before encouraged a reporter to drop a story that he believed in, but he also knew the Red Jackal survived best as a rumor. Let criminals fear the unknown; let them think that he might just be a figment of their imaginations.

And he couldn't exactly ask for help with the ethical quandary. Perhaps he could write a letter to *Editor & Publisher*: "Dear Sirs, I am a newspaper publisher but also a crusading crimefighter who wants to preserve his secret identity. How do I balance the two?"

The thought made him smile slightly, an expression that the fiery reporter mistook as aimed at her.

"I know, I know," Blake said, raising his hands as he sought to preemptively calm his top scribe. "Listen, find me proof. Get me evidence that this guy exists. Even a reliable eyewitness. Then we can talk. But I'm not publishing anything based on hearsay from crooks and mobsters. And be careful who you have dinner with."

Jennifer's mischievous grin returned. "I'm going to find it, Chief. Don't you worry. And if you're so worried about my dinner companions –"

Jennifer was cut off as Kate, Blake's gray-haired, long-time assistant leaned in the office door.

"You have a call, Mr. Randolph. It's Mr. Moore – he said it's an emergency."

"Thanks, Kate. I'll take it in here."

"Hmm, saved by the bell, I guess," Jennifer said with a sarcastic frown, immediately regretting her words when she saw the look on Blake's face.

"Wait, Rob … slow down. You're not making any sense. … How did … alright, I'm coming down now."

"Blake, what is it?" the concerned reporter asked, putting her hand on Blake's arm.

Blake was already heading out the door as he answered. "That was Rob Moore. His star pitcher is dead."

IV
That evening

YOU WILL *be blessed and you will be cursed. You will have great power and strength.*

It had been more than a decade since Blake had heard those words and he still wasn't sure it was worth the trade-off. True, nobody else had returned from the expedition, but at what cost? What had he given up for this cursed blessing?

Motion near the entrance of the alley shook him out of his reverie. *Focus on the task at hand.*

After meeting Moore at his office, it hadn't taken long to fill in the gaps. The Vermilion Bay Resort's star pitcher went out looking for some fun and got himself killed. The body, stripped of money and valuables, had been found in this alley near the Hopkins. The police had dismissed it as a robbery, just another rube who didn't know better than to watch himself in the city.

The server at the Hopkins's lounge was a recent hire by the name of Tim O'Rourke. He said that Josh had been buying drinks – beer and wine only, he assured the officers – for the crowd in the hotel bar and generally flashing his new-found wealth. The assumption was that someone had decided to lure him out to the alley and take that money for himself. Then, the theory went, the country bumpkin decided to fight to keep his cash and came out on the losing end of a gunshot.

It was a nice, clean package, tied up with a ribbon for the local constabulary.

Still, there had been no blood, no evidence to suggest he had been killed here, a fact conveniently ignored by the investigating officers. New reform-minded police officers and leadership were trying to clean up decades of corruption in the city, but much of the police force was still willing to take a payoff in the right situation.

Blake's intuition – almost superhuman since that night in

Egypt – told him it was worth coming back to the scene. It seemed that informed hunch had been right. The setting sun had left the alley mostly in shadow, but he had no trouble making out a figure slinking down the alley. The Red Jackal leapt from his perch atop the fire escape and landed behind the presumably homeless man, cutting off any avenue of egress.

"Wha--?" the man squealed in fear at the sudden appearance of the Jackal's scarlet cloak and jackal insignia, known to all those who made their lives on the streets of the Twin Cities.

"Be calm, friend. The innocent have nothing to fear from the Red Jackal," he said, looking the man square in his rheumy eyes.

"Nothing to fear ..." the vagrant whispered, mostly to himself.

"You were here last night," the Jackal continued, "when the young man's body was left in this alley. What did you see?"

The man answered in a monotone: "Two men dragged him in here. I thought it was one of the hotel dicks coming to kick me out again. They don't like when I come back here, but there's good eats coming out the back door there. ... So I got myself down behind those boxes," he said, gesturing at a pile of six or seven broken wooden crates at the end of the alley.

"Did you recognize the men? Did they say anything?"

"Never saw them before. But they said 'Creepy' wanted them to make it look like someone robbed him for his roll."

The Jackal grimaced at the comment. "I knew there was more to this than that bartender said. Cooper. That animal is a scourge to this entire community."

Harry "Creepy" Cooper – so dubbed because of his sinister smile – was the leader of the infamous Cooper Gang. Known as Coop to his gang members, Cooper had led the group on a rampage across the Midwest including bank robberies, murders and more. Whenever the heat elsewhere got to be too much, Cooper and his gang hid out in St. Paul thanks to a police force that was all too happy to look the other way. If Creepy was involved in this, then Josh had stumbled into something huge. He knew where he had to head next.

The Jackal turned his attention back to the helpful tramp.

"Take this, my good man," he said, handing the man five dollars. "Get yourself a warm bed and a meal. It's going to be chilly tonight."

The Jackal disappeared in a flash of red motion before the man could even acknowledge the gift. Within seconds, his memory of the Red Jackal was fading, even as the words "warm bed, warm meal," continued to repeat themselves in his mind.

V

WITHIN MINUTES, the Red Jackal had shed his outfit and transformed himself once again, using one of the many hideaways he kept for just such an occasion. Dressed smartly for an evening out on the town, Blake headed back to the Hopkins, this time through the front door.

He had taken the precaution of putting some gray in his hair and adding a moustache that should help keep anyone from recognizing him. Although not previously a patron of the Hopkins, his plan called for passing himself off as an out-of-town hood. It wouldn't do for a casual acquaintance to scotch his efforts.

As Blake entered the lounge he made a note of the sparse crowd. Most alcoholic drinks were still illegal, but tolerated here in the waning days of prohibition. One couple was whispering sweet nothings to each other at a table in the back corner, mostly hidden by shadows. At the bar, two other men sat, separated by three stools. The word of the murder seemed to have thinned out the crowd, with nobody eager to wind up as the next victim.

Blake picked a seat at the other end of the bar and motioned to the barkeep: "Scotch."

The bartender nodded and reached under the counter. When he brought the drink over, Blake grabbed his arm, holding it in an iron grip.

"Creepy wants to know what you were pulling with the cops today, O'Rourke," he said in a voice too low for any of the other patrons to hear.

A look of fear flashed across the barman's craggy face, confirming Blake's suspicion that he knew more than he had told the police that morning.

"I didn't say nothin' but what those boys told me," he whispered. "Just said he was flashing his money around."

Blake pulled on the old man's arm, almost dragging him across the counter, before offering a harsh whisper in his face.

"That's not what we heard. The flatfoots told us you couldn't stop singing once they put a little pressure on you."

"No, no," the bartender practically whimpered. "They let it go – hardly any questions. I didn't say nothing about The Pines."

"The Pines. Of course," Blake said under his breath, while releasing the man's arm. "Where better for a visitor with a wad of money to go waste it?"

A suspicious look crept into the barman's face at that comment. "Hey, how come I've never seen you with the crew before? What's your name?"

"You can call me Eliot Ness," Blake answered with a smile. "And I never said I worked for Creepy."

With space between them, the old man was now trying to regain a modicum of courage. "You won't get away with this. I don't know who you are, but Coop will take care of you."

Blake chuckled, then turned serious as he responded: "Sure, buddy. You want to know who I am? I'm a treasury agent, friend. So why don't you call Creepy up and tell him you just spilled your guts to a G-Man?" He gave the barman his best predatory smile.

With that, he slid off the stool and made his way to the bar's exit. He glanced back at the barkeep as he strode out the door, feeling a little sorry about the look of dawning terror on the man's face … but just a little.

VI

THE PINES. The sprawling mansion was a frequent destination for Cooper and his gang whenever they were in town.

The three-story home on the edge of St. Paul was a notorious gangland hangout. Gangsters and local high society rubbed elbows at its bars and gambling tables. Regular payoffs to St. Paul's police force made sure the illegal casino operation stayed up and running.

Ben Weaver, a bellhop turned underworld banker, ran the joint. The diminutive Minnesota native had made a successful business out of not only entertaining criminals both local and foreign, but also providing alibis for any hooligan that needed them – for a healthy fee.

Weaver was an expert at keeping his mouth shut. Blake knew he wasn't likely to share any information about whatever had prompted the need to eliminate Josh, even if the Jackal entered the picture. He wasn't cowardly enough to be tricked and intimidated like the bartender or pliable enough to be influenced like the tramp outside the Hopkins.

But every criminal operation has those people who just can't keep their mouths shut … which is why he was waiting outside this rundown tenement on the city's south side shortly before midnight. The doorway of the adjacent, boarded-up pharmacy made a convenient observation post.

The front door opened and a small, hunched over man scurried out. Dan Finley, or Weasel Dan as he was known to most in the Twin Cities criminal class, moved his eyes from side to side as if expecting to be attacked at any moment. One look at the miscreant made clear to the observer how he got his nickname.

I do have to deal with the worst people, the Jackal thought as he stepped out of the doorway of the abandoned building.

"Good evening, Dan."

"Oh, God! You scared the hell out of me! Can't you just walk up to a person like a normal guy?"

Finley had been a not-always-willing member of the Jackal's network of informants for the last three years – ever since the vigilante had extricated him from a sticky situation involving some missing Canadian whiskey and Al Capone's operation. Apparently, Chicago gangsters don't take kindly to having high-quality liquor replaced with turpentine. Luckily for Finley, no one who knew about his switcheroo had survived the misunderstanding.

After his failed attempt to strike it rich on his own, Finley had returned to his position as a blackjack dealer at The Pines. Those duties let him listen in on plenty of conversations that proved interesting to the Jackal.

"We need to talk about your employer. You need to do some digging for me."

Finley kept walking down the quiet street. "Uh, uh. Now is not the best time. Everyone's really jumpy over there. Something's going on."

The Jackal sighed. "I *know* something's going on, Dan. That's why I need *you* to find out what it is. It's sort of what an informant does."

"Quiet! Nobody needs to hear that."

The Jackal gestured at the surrounding street and buildings.

"Dan, who is going to hear? Half the buildings on the street are empty. And anyone else who lives here is just a good, hard-working citizen trying to make it through the Depression. You are the only deviant out this late. And I can ensure you there is nobody around. Enhanced senses and all that," the Jackal added while gesturing at his head.

"But if you're that worried, why don't you just step into this lovely vestibule," he said, indicating the doorway of another abandoned building.

Finley stopped with an exasperated grunt. "Fine, but make it quick. I start at 12."

"Last night ..."

"I was off last night."

"Yes, Dan, I know. More listening, less talking, and you can get on your way.

"I need you to find out about a kid named Josh Jacobson. At some point last night he made it over to The Pines, then somehow managed to end up dead in an alley next to the Hopkins Hotel. He was a ballplayer, just got a big signing bonus to play for a team up north and was probably spreading money around at the tables."

"Not to point out the obvious, but our average customer is not exactly an upstanding member of society. Somebody probably saw all that money and figured they'd bushwhack the kid."

"No, there's something more going on here than a simple robbery. Creepy is involved."

Finley's eyes opened wide. "You couldn't lead with that nugget? That guy's a nut job. If he's involved it could be just about anything."

The Jackal nodded. "I know. That's why you make the big money for all the answers."

"Wait – you don't pay me!"

"Call in at 10. Find out what this kid stumbled into."

As if he had conjured it out of thin air, a black, heavily modified Packard sedan appeared out of the darkness, running with no lights on. Within seconds, the Jackal had leapt into the backseat and the vehicle vanished back into the gloom.

"God, I hate when he does that," Finley said as he resumed scuffling down the street.

VII

BY 9:45 A.M. the next day, Blake was back in his office at the *Gazette*, discussing the case with his younger brother David and Rob Moore.

"The detectives won't say it, but I think they're done," Moore said. "Wrong place, wrong time and too much money to be throwing around.

"Maybe they're right," he continued with a resigned sigh. "But it doesn't feel right. Something's off. I don't know. Either way he's dead, but ... I just wish I had something to tell his sister. Even if it's just for her, I'd like to get to the bottom of this. I'm thinking of hiring a private dick to look into it."

"Sure, sure, that's an idea," Blake replied. "We have plenty of contacts from our work here at the paper and over at the brickyard. Why don't you let us take care of finding someone for you? David, look into that, why don't you?"

"Uh, yeah. I'll take care of it," David responded, sounding a little unsure of himself.

Moore ran his hands through his hair, accentuating his receding hairline and tired features.

"Alright, thanks guys. I've got to get going anyway. Josh's sister is arriving at Union Depot soon. She's coming down to claim the body and I told her I would help with funeral arrangements."

"Try to get some rest, too, Rob," Blake said as the portly man made his way out of the office. "I know it seems dark now, but don't give up. You've got a lot of friends here for you."

After Moore had left, closing the door behind him, David glanced over at his brother: "I assume I should belay that order to find a detective?"

"Yes, let's put it off for a couple of days at least," Blake replied. "It could very well prove unnecessary."

"I take that to mean the Red Jackal is making some progress?"

David, 12 years Blake's junior, was one of the few people who knew of his double life as publisher and crimefighter. The junior Randolph had recently graduated from the University of Chicago and returned to help run the Randolph businesses – and assist in other family endeavors.

"I think so. I've got Dan Finley checking things out at The Pines. I hope to hear an update any minute," he said, glancing at his watch.

"On another note, big brother, have you given any more thought to my proposal? I think the numbers work on the new antenna. We'd have a much larger audience and could charge a lot more for the advertising. Senator Charles thinks we can get the permits we need."

"There's potential there. I'll give you that, but I still need to look at everything. It's a big investment to make in an uncertain time ..."

The rest of his response was cut off by the buzzing of the closed-circuit communicator in his desk, which offered a direct line back to the Randolph family estate on the outskirts of Brickton.

"Yes Geoffrey?" Blake said as he grabbed the handset from out of his second drawer.

Geoffrey Stone was not only Blake's valet and driver, but also a veteran of Great Britain's Foreign Intelligence Service during the Great War.

"Yes, sir," he responded in his precise British accent. "That call you were expecting at 10 came in as scheduled. The party said that he has found a, err, solution to the problem you have been attempting to address. He's requested an immediate meeting to discuss his intelligence. He also mentioned the subject of remuneration, sir."

"Yes, I'm sure he did, Geoffrey. Thank you. Call him back and tell him to meet me at location 12-B at noon."

"I assume you will be needing the car and my services again?"

"Yes, meet me outside the *Gazette* in 20 minutes."

"Of course, sir. I will be there with the utmost speed."

Blake turned back to David as he hung up the phone.

"Well, Dan's got something. Looks like the Red Jackal has another meeting. Can you ..."

"... take care of the afternoon staff meeting? Of course. And remember to watch your back, Blake. His nickname's not Weasel Dan *only* because of his looks."

VIII

IN ORDER to better hide his identity from his enemies and his network of informants, the Red Jackal kept a number of locations across the Twin Cities for clandestine meetings. Coded names and numbers, known only to his associates, also helped to keep those meeting places secret.

The Depression had, unfortunately, provided a wealth of abandoned buildings to choose from. Location 12-B, the site for the Jackal's meeting with Weasel Dan, was the basement of an empty office building near the state capitol building in St. Paul.

The Jackal was already waiting there by the time Finley arrived for their noon meeting. Geoffrey and the car were well-hidden nearby, ready to be signaled at a moment's notice.

"What do you have for me, Dan?" the Jackal asked as Finley entered through the shadowy doorway.

"Something's happening. I hear Creepy showed up for a few minutes two nights ago and met with Weaver ..."

"The same night Josh was killed," the Jackal mused.

"Yeah, sounds like it. Anyway, he had a meeting with Weaver in his office, but otherwise ain't nobody seen him around The Pines for about a week.

"But here's the big news: The gang has a big score planned – hundreds of thousands of dollars."

That amount stunned the Jackal. This was no simple bank robbery, an observation he shared with Finley. His assumption had been a holdup or hijacking of some sort was on the docket – the Cooper gang was well known for their bank heists. They had left a trail of dead and wounded bank guards across the Midwest, hitting dozens of local banks.

"Are you sure they weren't exaggerating? Where'd you get that?"

"All the Borkis brothers are in town. You know how Albert likes to talk when he starts drinking. He was blabbing away at the table until Fred showed and told him to clam up."

Affiliates of the Cooper gang, the Borkis family only came in on the biggest heists. They had been rumored to be hiding out in the northwoods of Wisconsin following a bungled robbery of the reserve bank in St. Louis. The debacle had left six employees and two police officers dead – and the Borkises with no reward from the heist. Albert Borkis was the youngest and dumbest of the boys.

"So, they're bringing in the muscle," the Jackal mused. "The Borkis Boys. That's one family tree you don't want to climb."

From a family of backwoods bootleggers in the Ozarks, the six Borkis boys were big, strong, mean – and not too bright. Nobody was really sure if the boys were brothers, cousins or both – including them.

"Whatever it is, that means Creepy is trying to keep his guys out of it and let the Borkis boys do the dirty work. Did you get anything else from Albert? A location, a name, anything?"

"I don't know. Albert was pretty far gone. He was talking about a lot of stuff that didn't make sense and I was trying not to be too obvious that I was paying attention. I think he said something about a farm in California."

"California? I don't think the Borkis boys have ever been west of the Dakotas. This is getting odder and odder. OK, think about it. Did any of the other boys say anything?"

Finley crinkled his eyes in thought.

"You know ... Johnny was going after one of the waitresses pretty hard. She gave him the brush off and he said she wouldn't do that next week. Maybe that means somethin'?"

"I'd wager it means he's expecting a big payday, but how?"

THE RED Jackal spent the rest of that day checking in with informants across the Cities, becoming increasingly frustrated. There was little doubt that something big was in the wind. Most of the Cooper gang had gone underground – nowhere to be seen. The more deplorable citizens of the metropolis were abuzz with the news of the Borkis boys' arrival in town, although no one seemed to know where they were hiding out, either.

It was a stark departure for Harry Cooper, who loved the attention he got by going out on the town. Whether it was The Pines, the 5-8 Club in Minneapolis or some other mob hangout, it was rare to see the night when Creepy didn't show up with a new beauty on his arm. *For someone with that well-deserved nickname, he does remarkably well with the opposite sex.*

The work continued after dark, as the Jackal roamed the mean streets of St. Paul. While he did manage to break up the robbery of a liquor store and thwart two muggings, he didn't get any closer to a solution.

By 1 a.m. he had retrieved the Packard and returned to the Brickton estate. Sleep eluded him even at that late hour.

IX

BETTER EQUIPPED than the average man to handle a sleepless night, Blake Randolph was up and having his breakfast by 7 a.m. the next morning, as was his habit.

Despite his frequent nocturnal activities, Randolph almost always drank his coffee and ate his morning meal at that time. It was also usually his only opportunity to peruse the region's morning papers before getting caught up in the regular doings of the newsroom. It was a schedule that was rarely modified and one that Geoffrey protected unless imperative business interfered.

That was why Blake ignored the phone when it rang – and knew the day was not going to get off to a good start when he saw Geoffrey standing in the doorway of the dining room.

"I do apologize, sir, but Mr. Stanley is on the phone for you. He insists it is an emergency."

Rod Stanley was the *Gazette's* long-time city editor and the man who kept the newsroom going. It was newsmen like Stanley they had in mind when the phrase "ink running in his veins" was coined.

"Well, let's see what our illustrious city editor needs. I'll take it in here," he said, reaching for the telephone handset.

"Good morning, Rod. What's going on?"

"It's a big one, boss. All hell's breaking loose at the St. Paul police headquarters. No official confirmation yet, but we're hearing that Elaine Sullivan was kidnapped last night."

Blake slammed his hand down on the dining table.

"Kidnapped? Dammit, that must be ..."

"What boss? I can't hear you. It's crazy down here."

"Nothing, Rod. Who do you have chasing it?"

"Jennifer Jones is already down at headquarters."

"Alright. If anyone can get to the straight dope, it's her. I'm coming down."

Elaine Sullivan – the 25-year-old heir to the Sullivan's Department Store fortune. Sullivan's was Minnesota's answer to Marshall Field's, with its flagship store a downtown St. Paul landmark. Sullivan's father was one of the wealthiest men in Minnesota.

It seemed clear just what the young pitcher had stumbled into at The Pines – the question was whether it was too late to do anything about it.

"STILL NOTHING official, but I've got off-the-record confirmation that it's true," Jennifer Jones' voice said over the telephone. "I'm also hearing there's already been a ransom demand: $250,000."

"OK, Miss Jones, good work. Keep at it," Stanley responded.

"A quarter million dollars!" Stanley exclaimed after both men had hung up their handsets in Blake's office.

"Well, if anyone can afford that, it's Sullivan, but even for him that's a pretty penny," Blake observed. "Still, it's a big risk. You might be able to get some of the St. Paul cops to look the other way on minor stuff, but this is pretty big. And isn't Sullivan friends with the president?"

"That's right," Stanley replied. "Sullivan was a big supporter last fall and at the convention. That's going to mean lots of pressure."

"OK, keep on it, Rod. Let me know if anything else breaks."

No wonder Creepy farmed this one out, Blake thought as Stanley left his office. *The heat's going to be incredible.*

I'm missing something. It's right there … They've got to take the Sullivan kid somewhere. They're not going to hide her at The Pines. Anywhere in St. Paul or Minneapolis is too hot … across the river to

Wisconsin? The country somewhere, anyway. And what does California have to do with it?

"Oh my god!" He reached for the communicator in his desk, using his direct line to Geoffrey.

"Geoffrey, we need to track down Dan Finley right now. He usually eats breakfast with the other overnight employees at Casey's Diner."

Luckily, Finley was a creature of habit. Within 10 minutes, Geoffrey had him on the line.

"You know who this is?" Blake said, changing his voice to the deeper version he used when in his guise as the Red Jackal.

"Yeah, it's the –"

"Stop right there. Think very hard, Dan. Are you absolutely sure Albert Borkis said 'a farm in California' the other night?"

"Yeah, sure. It seemed weird to me, but …"

"Were those his exact words? Or did he say San Francisco?"

"Well, yeah, but San Francisco's in California, right? I didn't know they had farms there, but I've never been west of Lake Minnetonka."

"Oh, Dan. You idiot. Pick up a map. There's a San Francisco township in Carver County. It's nothing but farms!"

"Huh, what do you know. I wonder why they call it that?"

But there was no response as Blake had already slammed down the phone.

X

THE SUN setting over the farmhouse off of State Highway 41 would have made a pretty picture at another time. As it was, for the Red Jackal it was only an impediment to the coming darkness. With his enhanced senses, darkness was a friend to the Jackal.

In retrospect, it had been relatively easy to find the old dairy farm. By late afternoon, Geoffrey's efforts had uncovered a handful of potential sites. The Jackal's reconnaissance of those locations identified this operation, which had far too much activity for a farm that had been repossessed by the bank.

He had left Geoffrey at the estate to coordinate his efforts. with instructions to notify local authorities if he didn't hear from the Jackal within two hours. The Packard was hidden a quarter-mile away, just off the highway.

The last several hours had convinced him that the only ones on site were the six Borkis boys, at least for now. He mentally reviewed the layout of the farm: *Red barn, about 300 feet away; black Lincoln, just outside the barn. One guard with the cars. White farmhouse, another 500 feet or so from the barn, with front and back doors; curtains blocking any view into or out of the windows. Outhouse, 100 feet behind the back door.*

Within minutes, the darkness of the moonless night was almost complete. The Jackal crept from his hiding spot at the tree line across the open field to the back of the barn. Working quickly, he slipped through a gap in the wall he had spotted earlier. Once inside the barn, he stopped to listen. Not a sound. No one in the barn, as he had suspected. But it wasn't empty. Two Ford V-8-powered 18s were hidden inside. He slipped a short knife from his boot and made short work of the whitewall tires.

Exiting the same way he had entered, the Jackal made his way to the front corner of the barn. The glowing eye of a cigarette gave away the location of the guard posted to watch the cars. With one swift leap, the Jackal was on him. Covering his mouth and cutting off his air supply, the Jackal had him unconscious before he could raise an alarm. He turned over the unsuccessful watchman and recognized him as Benny Borkis.

"Alright, Benny, let's find somewhere to keep you out of the way." Binding his wrists, the Jackal dragged the criminal into the barn. "You know, Benny, it wouldn't kill you to take a bath every once in a while."

After depositing the malodorous gangster, he returned to

disable the Lincoln and grab Benny's shotgun.

One down, five to go.

With the darkness hiding his movement, the Jackal silently moved to the rear of the house, positioning himself in bushes near the outhouse. *Time to wait for nature to call.* He had noticed earlier in the day that the Borkises were using the outhouse regularly, so either there wasn't indoor plumbing in the farmhouse or it wasn't working. It only took a few minutes for one of the Borkis boys to emerge from the back door and make their way to the latrine.

Before the door closed, the Jackal managed to get a good look inside: three men, all sitting at a kitchen table, beers and cards in front of them. When the unknown Borkis finished his business and emerged from the outhouse, the Jackal delivered a swift blow to the temple with the stock of Benny's shotgun. He quickly glanced at the house to be sure no one there had heard anything. It seemed he had been quiet enough.

He searched the unconscious man, finding two knives and a Smith & Wesson .38 Special. He deposited those and the shotgun into the depths of the outhouse hole, then pulled the Borkis into the small building. *Still smells better than Benny.*

He had just finished doing that when the back door flew open.

"Eli, where the hell are you?" came the yell from the back steps.

"I'm fregging hetting," the Jackal said from the backyard, intentionally unintelligible.

"What are you talking about? Fred wants you back inside," he said as he continued walking toward the small outbuilding.

Albert Borkis glanced up just in time to see a blur of motion from the large maple tree.

"Huh," he blurted as the Jackal knocked him to the ground. As the unconscious Albert fell to the grass, his finger pulled the trigger of the Tommy gun in his hand. With the element of surprise gone, the Jackal didn't bother to incapacitate Albert, only pausing to throw his gun into the underbrush.

He charged the back door of the house, Browning .45 drawn and ready. As he burst into the kitchen, he found two more Tommy guns aimed in his direction. A quick shot to the right hit one of the remaining Borkis boys in the chest and he swiftly moved to the left to take care of the second.

"Tommy!" he heard as he pulled the trigger and felt a bulk slam into him, spilling him over and knocking the .45 from his hand. It also caused the shot to go off target, hitting Fred Borkis in the shoulder. As he went down, he saw the open basement door behind him from which Johnny Borkis had emerged.

Johnny delivered a swift blow to his midsection, but his follow-up punch slammed into the floor when the Jackal rolled out of the way. The Jackal sprang up as Johnny yowled in pain, delivering a roundhouse kick that sent the oldest Borkis sprawling on the floor. The Jackal glanced around for his .45 or another weapon, even as Johnny pulled his own knife and charged.

The Jackal deflected the attack with his armored wrist, then grabbed Johnny's arm, twisting until Johnny's fingers slipped off the knife. Screaming, Johnny launched himself at the Jackal, fingers searching for a grip on the vigilante's throat. The Jackal easily slipped the attack and pivoted around behind Johnny. Johnny charged, while the Jackal sidestepped the attack. Too late, Johnny realized he was headed for the open basement door. He tried to stop, but slipped on a spot of blood, screaming as he plummeted to the cellar floor.

One glance at the unnatural angle of Johnny's neck at the bottom of the stairs told the Jackal all he needed to know. He turned his attention to the other two Borkis boys in the room. Tommy was dead as well from his gunshot. Fred, on the other hand, while unconscious from the blood loss, would survive if he received medical care soon.

"MMHHMM!"

That was coming from the basement. The Jackal moved carefully down the stairs to discover Elaine Sullivan, bound and gagged on an old wooden chair.

"Miss Sullivan," he said, as he removed her gag. "I think you're safe now."

"Who are you?" she asked cautiously, eyeing his mask and the blood on his clothing.

"You can say I'm a friend. I would advise you to close your eyes as we leave. It got a bit messy up there."

With no Borkis boys to get in the way, the return trip to the Packard was uneventful, with only a quick stop to tie up Albert Borkis and toss him in the outhouse. A quick call to Geoffrey over the car's radio had the Carver County Sheriff's Department dispatched. By the time they arrived to arrest the four surviving gangsters, the Jackal and his charge were long gone.

XI

AS IT turned out, the kidnappers had treated Elaine Sullivan remarkably well. She had been fed regularly and not been mistreated in any way – if one ignored the ropes and gag.

She shared her story with the Jackal as he drove her back into the city, heading toward her St. Paul home. It was well-known that the fiercely independent Elaine, much to her father's dismay, volunteered regularly at soup kitchens and other establishments with similar goals. She had been leaving a mission in the Gateway District of Minneapolis when three men grabbed her and threw her in the back of a car. They had driven just a few blocks, then switched to one of the Fords the Jackal had seen at the San Francisco farm. They had immediately driven to the farm, where she had since been confined in the farmhouse's cellar.

"I must say, Miss Sullivan, I'm impressed by your resilience. I've seen so-called tough guys fall apart under those conditions."

"And I'm just a poor little woman?" she said sharply.

"No offense meant, Miss Sullivan. I have the utmost respect for what you do and your obvious strength."

"A nice compliment from the Red Jackal," Sullivan replied as they neared her family's Summit Avenue mansion.

The Jackal was thrown by the sudden shift in subject. "Uh, well …"

"You can't do what I do and not have heard of the Red Jackal. And the mask and suit are a bit of a giveaway. The lone hero fighting a corrupt system. For the people I work with, you're a hero."

"Well, I appreciate that, but I prefer to keep a low profile. I would appreciate discretion."

He slowed down and pulled to the side of the street, before turning to look at the young woman.

"Speaking of which," he said, gesturing in the direction of her home. "It appears there is quite a bit of police attention to your abode. It would be most helpful to me if I could drop you off this short distance away."

"Well, then, I suppose I can say it was some unknown hero who rescued me and dropped me off. 'As a poor distraught woman, I really can't remember anything that happened.'"

"Something tells me that few people who know you will accept that."

"Well, it will be good enough for the papers. Until we meet again, Red Jackal," Elaine Sullivan said with an enigmatic smile as she exited the Packard.

"*AND NO* sign of Creepy?" David asked

"No, it appears he skipped town ahead of any consequences. It's been two days and nobody's seen hide nor hair," Blake said. "The authorities seem to have no interest in putting much effort into finding him for that matter."

The brothers were once again in the offices of the Gazette, discussing the Jackal's latest adventure. The Borkis boys had been arrested by Carver County deputies and turned over to the St. Paul authorities. Their expensive mouthpiece was working to get them sprung from jail, citing the unorthodox arrests.

"And the Red Jackal?"

Blake smiled. "It seems his involvement has thus far remained unacknowledged. Miss Sullivan has been good to her word and it appears the Borkis boys have clammed up as well."

A sharp rapping came at the door of Blake's office. Before either brother could even acknowledge the knock, Jennifer Jones rushed in.

"OK, chief. This time you've got to let me run with it. I'm hearing the Red Jackal was the one who rescued Elaine Sullivan from that farm. I've got two sources that ..."

David grinned to himself, stood up and headed out the door.

"I'll be leaving you to deal with this, big brother. Good luck."

He was still smiling as he made his way out of the newsroom and looked back to see Blake Randolph trapped in his office by the intrepid reporter.

A Tip of the Cowl

As any aficionado of Minnesota crime history probably recognizes, this story has a basis in real-life events. The corruption in the police forces in both of the Twin Cities at the time was, unfortunately, all too real.

It may be a surprise to those who think of "Minnesota Nice" today, but in the 1920s and '30s, St. Paul and Minneapolis were rife with crime and corruption. Criminals from John Dillinger to Ma Barker to Babyface Nelson spent time in the area whenever the heat got too bad in other parts of the country.

That was thanks to the "layover agreement" or "O'Connor System" in place from 1900 to the 1930s. Named for St. Paul Police Chief John J. O'Connor, the deal effectively gave the criminals freedom to hide out in St. Paul in exchange for the promise that they would check in with police officials when they arrived in the city, wouldn't commit crimes in the city and would share a portion of their ill-gotten gains.

The system continued even past O'Connor's 1920 retirement, through the prohibition era.

The Sullivan kidnapping in *Dead Ball* was inspired by two kidnappings in the Twin Cities of brewer William Hamm Jr. (in 1933) and banker Edward Bremer (in 1934). With the end of prohibition in 1933, and the growing efforts by J. Edgar Hoover's fledgling Federal Bureau of Investigation to take out gangsters, criminals were getting increasingly desperate.

The real-life kidnappers took their victims to Bensenville, Illinois, a Chicago suburb where they hid out until getting their ransom payments. For the purposes of this tale, I chose to keep the kidnapping "local." And for those of you not familiar with Carver County, both it and the unincorporated town of San Francisco, Minnesota, are quite real.

In real life, both Hamm and Bremer were eventually released unharmed after the payment of large ransoms.

Still, the publicity engendered by the cases is largely credited with bringing down the corrupt members of the St. Paul Police Department and ending the "O'Connor agreement" that had allowed out-of-town gangsters to get a free pass in the city. By the mid-1930s, most of the old guard of the St. Paul Police Department was gone, replaced by more reform-minded officers and leadership.

Murder

Transcribed

The Red Jackal has to fight death on the airwaves when life imitates art!

I

OLE KARLSSON cursed the sun as it rose over Lake Superior that bright July morning. He also cursed Anders Lindberg for the alcohol he had given him the previous evening.

"Canadian whiskey, my ass," he said to the dog trotting beside him. "That *skulor* was whipped up in somebody's bathtub, Hoover."

Ole squinted as he continued up the hill to the Forest Park Cemetery, where he worked as the caretaker. The cemetery, the oldest in Duluth – at least the oldest *white* cemetery – overlooked the lake. At a different time and without a pounding headache, Ole would have found the sunrise beautiful. Most mornings Ole was happy to have this job. He got to work outside and he enjoyed the irony that a poor immigrant got to look down over the city as he toiled. It beat working in one of the iron ore mines like many of his fellow newcomers to the state ... or standing in the bread line.

While he had seriously considered staying in bed to nurse his hangover, he knew there were plenty of men who would be more than happy to take his job.

"Come on, Hoover," Ole said to the dog who had become something of a mascot for the employees of the cemetery. One of the gravediggers had suggested the name when the dog showed up two years earlier, joking that he was probably homeless thanks to the president. When the dog kept returning, the name stuck. Eventually, Hoover had ended up living with Ole.

He grimaced as he approached the main gate to the cemetery, seeing that it stood slightly open. He was sure he had locked up the night before when leaving for the day, but maybe he had forgotten? *No*, he thought, shaking his head and wincing as it started pounding again. *Damn you Anders.*

There had been trouble with vandals at some of the other cemeteries in Duluth, so Ole feared the worst. He examined the gate, but it didn't appear to be broken or damaged. Perhaps he *had* simply forgotten to close it. *Still, better check things out.*

He quickened his pace, heading toward the shed where the crew kept all of their tools and other supplies for maintaining the cemetery. He saw with relief that the building was still locked. A quick look inside confirmed that nothing was missing or damaged. He set down his thermos and filled up Hoover's water bowl, then sighed. As comfortable as the dark, cool shed was, Ole

knew he couldn't put off the inevitable.

"Well, Hoover, time to see if we had any trouble here last night." Ole started to head out the door, then reversed himself and grabbed a shovel off the wall. "We might need this, boy."

He stepped back outside, blinking in the bright sunlight and dreading walking the full acreage of the cemetery. In all likelihood, though, he expected any trouble probably occurred near the front of the cemetery, the area with the most graves and closest to the gate.

He headed west first, figuring at least the sun would be at his back and not in his eyes.

After nearly half an hour, he had seen no signs of mischief. He noted with approval that flags were still evident throughout the cemetery, remnants of the July 4 service just two days earlier.

"Maybe we lucked out, Hoover," he said. As if in response, the dog let out a single bark and sprang off toward the woods running along the western edge of the cemetery.

"Get back here you dumb mutt!" Ole shouted.

Hoover had already crested the hill and was out of Ole's sight when he started barking repeatedly. "Probably just chasing a rabbit," Ole said to himself, not quite believing it.

"Hoover!"

If anything, the dog's barks got louder and more excited. As Ole ran up the hill, he saw Hoover barking and jumping excitedly around a cluster of graves in the oldest section of the cemetery. He slowed, feeling with a sudden sense of certainty that he didn't want to see what was behind those monuments.

I don't care what that stuff was, I could use another glass of it now.

He continued to slowly approach, but stopped when he saw a pair of shoes (and two legs) extending past the last gravestone in the row.

"Just a bum sleeping one off," he said, barely at a whisper.

Three more steps took him around the end of the row, where he could clearly see the ground in front of the graves. One look at the bulging eyes and open mouth told him the young man lying on the ground wasn't going to be sleeping anything off ever again.

I really should have stayed in bed was the last thing Ole thought before he passed out.

"You betrayed me, Willie. You know what happens to a traitor?"

"Frankie, it can't be. I thought you were dead!"

"I am dead, Frankie. Dead and buried here in the cemetery ... and you're the one who put me here. And now I'm taking you with me."

"No, no. Your hands ... stay away from me ..."

"I'll squeeze the life out of you, Frankie. I'll choke out your last breath!"

"AHHHHHH!!!!"

THUMP!

"Over here, officer. This is where I heard the yelling. Sounded like

*someone was getting killed. Right over here ... what's that behind that
gravestone. It looks like ... a body!"*

*"It's a body alright. That's Frankie Davis the mobster. Let me look
at him. Why, there's not a mark on him. He just looks like he was scared
to death! Like he seen a ghost ..."*

"Bwa-ha-ha-ha-ha! Hello again, this is your teller of tales on The
Murder Hour. *It seems Frankie learned that murder never pays ...
except in kind. Don't be scared ... tonight's story was just a story, a tale
designed to chill and thrill. After all, such things don't happen in real
life ... or do they? Bwa-ha-ha-ha-ha!"*

*"From the shores of Lake Superior to the dark streets of
Minneapolis, we bring you tales of murder and mayhem. And remember
those loud bangs you hear this week are certainly just fireworks
celebrating our nation's birthday, not gunshots ... probably. Bwa-ha-
ha-ha!"*

*"Be sure to join us again at 7 o'clock next Sunday night for another
episode of* The Murder Hour, *live from the KBGZ studios."*

A short balding man standing outside the glass recording
booth held up his finger for about thirty seconds as the music
swelled over the end credits of the broadcast.

"And we are clear," Keith Rogers said as he lowered his hand.
"Nice work everyone. Almost flawless. What did you think Mr.
Randolph?"

Rogers turned to look at the tall, dark-haired man sitting off
to the side. Blake Randolph, publisher, radio station owner,
business tycoon and – as only a few knew – the crime-fighting
Red Jackal.

"It sounded great to me, Keith, but you're the expert. All I can
say is I'm glad you talked me into this little experiment of yours."

"The Murder Hour" was the station's first attempt at original
scripted entertainment. With network shows on summer
vacation, Blake had agreed to let his station manager develop his
own summer replacement series. It had been an immediate
success and after only six weeks there was talk of the network
taking the show national. Quite an accomplishment for a small

city radio station competing for attention with the larger stations in nearby Minneapolis and St. Paul. A lucrative sponsorship agreement with local flour mill Glendon Mills was also bringing in plenty of cash for the station.

"Mr. Randolph?"

Blake turned to see Margaret O'Malley, Rogers' assistant and occasional on-air talent, standing on the other side of the room holding the phone. The 24-year-old, red-headed Irish Catholic was, as always, dressed conservatively, although he noticed the chain she usually wore with a gold crucifix was inside her dress rather than outside today.

"It's the *Gazette* newsroom. They say they need to talk to you."

The newsroom was three floors down from the radio station in the *Gazette* building, the tallest in Brickton. As Blake took the phone, he watched Rogers step into the recording booth where Kent Franklin was wiping the sweat from his brow. The local stage actor had proven to be a natural at radio, and was playing most of the male voices on the new show, including four different characters tonight.

He found Rod Stanley on the other end of the line. The city editor told him they had a reporter chasing a late story and he needed to know if they could push back the presses 30 minutes. The extra wait would potentially put the printers into overtime pay. As he listened to Rod explain the story, he noticed that the director and actor appeared to be yelling at each other in the soundproof booth.

Blake told Rod to move the press time back, then hung up and quickly moved back over to the recording booth. The men moved out of the booth just as he reached it.

"Hey, Kent we rehearsed it several times today," Rogers said. "It's not my fault you didn't show up until 30 minutes before we went on the air. You were supposed to be here at one o'clock. I almost had to have Harrison play your part!"

At the sound of his name, Harrison Chase glanced up

nervously, and pushed his glasses back as they slipped down his nose. A short, acne-scarred twentyish man, Chase was a glorified gofer at the station who made occasional appearances on the air. He was determined to carve out a career on the air, but in the six months since he had arrived from Hermantown, he hadn't accomplished much besides making mediocre coffee and learning how to fix all the equipment.

"Go ahead and put the kid on the air. What do I care? With a face like that, he's meant for radio."

Chase flushed at that and went back to collecting the script pages that were scattered all over the floor.

"Kent …" Rogers said, a warning tone on his voice.

"Did I sound like I needed to rehearse? Did I make a mistake?"

"That's not the point! You're not the only member of this cast. We're a team here and —"

"Team? Please, I'm the one who makes this show work. Forget it – I've got a real play to rehearse for," he said pushing past Rogers and out the door. Rogers made a disgusted grunt and slammed his right hand on the glass wall of the booth.

"What was that all about?" Blake asked.

"Usual actor garbage. Franklin's buying his own hype. He's getting offers to leave our, as he put it, 'Midwest cow town' and work in Chicago or New York. He's the star and he's not afraid to let us know it. This has been going on for a couple weeks now, and it's getting worse. He shows up late or drunk, or both most of the time. I've had just about enough of him. As far as I'm concerned the sooner he's gone, the better."

Blake nodded in the direction of Harrison Chase. "Is he really the backup plan, then?"

Rogers shrugged his shoulders. "Oh, I don't know. Most weeks he knows all the scripts and he does most of the small parts that Kent doesn't do. This week might have been tough because he went back home for the holiday, so he wasn't part of the rehearsals or anything, but the dirty little secret of radio is they don't have to memorize anything. It's not like the stage ...

"As much as I hate to admit, Franklin does have a star quality. Harrison is ... competent. He's not going to set the studio on fire, but he's not going to embarrass us either. We could do worse."

Blake chuckled deeply. "That's what I always like to hear from my employees: we could do worse."

Rogers smiled. "Now you know why you pay me the medium money."

II

WORKING ON a Friday night ... this wasn't what he had planned on when he took a job as a bookkeeper for the Freeman Company, Bertrand James thought. But here he was, 39 years old, single and – at nearly 9 p.m. on a Friday – digging through papers on the 12th floor.

He paused to look out the window of the Armstrong Tower, with its unimpeded view of the starlit sky. There were some benefits to the job, he supposed. Thinking of benefits brought to mind Miss Idle, Mr. Freeman's secretary. Getting to see her in a form-fitting dress ... or one of those sweaters that hugged her rather ample bosom was usually the highlight of his day. Not that she noticed he existed, he thought. He bet *she* wasn't spending Friday night alone in the dark ...

Better not to think about it. Back to work, he thought.

He turned his attention back to the ledgers and papers on his desk, shaking his head in frustration. The Freeman Company was in financial trouble, but shouldn't be, Bertrand was convinced. He knew that sales of the company's cigarettes had only grown since the stock market crash. It seemed that smoking was one thing people weren't willing to give up. The company's board was set to meet next week and Bertrand would have to explain the numbers.

"Good luck with that when *I* can't even understand them," he muttered.

He took off his glasses and leaned back in his chair, rubbing his tired eyes. He was staring at the ceiling, letting his mind wander back to Miss Idle's curvaceous form, when he thought he saw a quick flash of movement out of the corner of his eye. He sat up quickly and peered out into the main office, but saw only the same shadows and lamps that had been there all night. The Freeman Company was the only business on the Armstrong's top three floors and Bertrand knew that he should be the only one in the office. He got out from behind his desk and moved quietly toward the doorway, straining to listen. Not a sound. Not a footstep, a creak or a groan.

"Just my nerves," the bespectacled accountant said as he returned to his desk, sure what he had thought was movement was just a trick of his failing eyes.

He dove back into the books, looking for an explanation for the company's struggles. After another 45 minutes without progress, he was about ready to give up for the night when he heard a scraping sound, perhaps like a chair being moved.

Bertrand briefly considered calling the police, but knew that if they arrived and found nothing he would never hear the end of it from the executives here at the Freeman Company. They already mocked him behind his back, he was sure. Salesmen with their slicked hair and fancy suits and dates on weekend nights. Especially that Griffith, asking him every Monday how his weekend was, asking how many books he had read. As if there was something wrong with reading.

At least I can read something more challenging than Dime Detective, *you witless ignoramus.* But of course he would never say that. Instead, he just took it every week, letting Griffith make his little jabs. He probably got plenty of women who looked like Miss Idle.

Enough of this. I'm going home.

He got up again and cautiously looked out his door. The outer office was empty, without a sign of life. He stepped out and slowly made his way across the large open floor where the secretarial pool worked, passing each desk with its typewriter covered up and stowed for the weekend. He had just about reached the elevator when he noticed a dim light coming from Mr. Freeman's office at the far end of the hall.

Was that lamp on earlier? He didn't think so, but it had also still been light out when he arrived at the office after dinner, so he may not have noticed.

Was that another noise? Now his ears were playing tricks on him, too. Just the sounds of a building settling after a hot day, he thought.

He considered just leaving and heading home, but what if something was missing from Mr. Freeman's office when he returned Monday morning? And people started asking why he was in the office Friday night? He might not like working for Freeman, but it was better than being unemployed. He didn't kid himself that there was a big demand for accountants these days.

Bertrand took a steadying breath and moved down the hall. He stopped outside the door, but heard nothing besides his own breathing. He stepped into the office and saw that there was a lamp glowing on Mr. Freeman's desk. He took two steps into the office before he felt a breeze of movement behind him. He screamed as he spun around, then laughed in relief as he saw a pigeon land on the bookcase against the wall, cocking its head as if wondering what this strange man was doing.

It was then that he noticed the door leading to Mr. Freeman's private balcony was slightly ajar. Well, that explained how the pigeon had gotten in and wreaked its havoc.

He opened the door wide, yelling, "Out! Out!" and waving his hands at the pigeon. With the uninvited guest gone, he stepped out on the balcony. As he rested both hands on the railing he laughed again, glad that no one else had been around to see him almost scare himself to death. Wouldn't that have been ammunition for Griffith and the rest!

He shook his head and breathed deeply, enjoying the cool evening after the hot, humid day. He had barely exhaled when he felt two strong hands grip him and easily flip him over the railing into the night air.

That's what I get for being brave, he thought as the pavement rushed up to meet him.

Sundays were the worst, Kent Franklin thought as he stood before the front door of his second-floor apartment shortly after 3 a.m. Women didn't want dates. There were no good parties. Even most of the speakeasies were closed.

That's why he tried to make Saturday night last as long as possible, but he had been escorted off the premises of the 5-8 Club after one of the bar girls decided she didn't want to be friendly anymore.

And worst of all, he was due at the studio this afternoon to deliver more of that dreck that passed for entertainment here in the sticks. He was a serious actor, damn it, trained in Shakespeare. But this lousy radio show might finally prove to be his ticket out of Minnesota. Even Chicago would be better. But New York – New York was where he belonged. He had been passed over time and again for opportunities to head east, all because he hadn't come from the right kind of family, because he had grown up poor in St. Paul's Swede Hollow neighborhood.

If that's what it took, he would ride this melodramatic crap all the way to Broadway.

At least he had gotten a chance to give Keith Rogers a piece of his mind earlier that day. The two had both ended up at the Chestnut Grille Saturday night. When he saw Rogers walk in with that secretary of his – of course that Margaret O'Malley would be out with him, Irish trash – he knew it was his chance to set the record straight. The result was a bit of a blur, but he had gotten at least one good punch in before Sweeney tossed him out.

He looked again at the door, trying to figure out why it wasn't open. He tried to turn the doorknob, but it was locked. *Maybe I did imbibe a little too much tonight*, he thought. *Or maybe I forgot to lock the door when I left.* He gripped the wavering knob with his left hand and carefully, slowly, guided the key into the lock with his right. This time he managed to unlock the door, and he stepped into the dark apartment.

"Well, that's better," he said closing the door behind him. He stumbled toward the center of his living room where the light from the street provided enough illumination that he could see the dim silhouette of the floor lamp.

"Light, seeking light, doth light of light ..." he bellowed in his stentorian stage voice, then devolved into drunken laughter.

He almost knocked the lamp over, but managed to catch it before it could hit the floor. He yanked on the pull chain but to no avail, trying to look more carefully but realizing that the swaying string was making him slightly dizzy. He grabbed it again, tugging with full force this time.

He barely had time to register the sound of the gunshot before he fell to the floor.

III

"WHERE IS Franklin?" Keith Rogers bellowed as he looked again at the clock on the studio wall and touched his bruised cheek. "We go live in six minutes!"

Margaret had just returned the phone to its cradle when she responded. "I just called downstairs. Still no sign of him."

Rogers ran his hand through what remained of his hair, then smacked his leg, wincing at the pain in his hand. *That drunken idiot,* he thought.

"This time he's pushed it too far," he said. "Enough is enough. I don't care if he is the star.

"Harrison!" he shouted to the young man who was pouring water glasses for the cast and checking the microphones before the broadcast started. Chase nearly spilled the water, jumping as Rogers yelled for him.

"Yes, sir, Mr. Rogers," he replied nervously as he hustled over to the director.

"If Franklin's not here in the next two minutes, you're going on the air. Looks like you're getting your shot, kid. Get in the booth."

"Uh, yes, sir!"

Chase ran to the booth, tripping over the door frame. Rogers closed his eyes and pressed his hand into his forehead, muttering, "God help us." More loudly, he spoke to the cast and crew: "We'll be fine, everyone, don't worry. Harrison's got the script and we've all done this before!

"But if anyone knows an appropriate prayer for the moment, now might be a good time!" he added with a smile. That comment caused a ripple of laughter to go through the group, as Rogers had hoped.

Chase knew the script, no doubt. He filled in for Franklin during rehearsal almost every week, but he didn't have that star quality. Franklin, for all his obnoxious behavior, had it, Rogers

knew. *Who knows? Maybe the kid won't be too bad. I always said it was my writing that was the star ...*

He glanced at the clock again. "OK, folks, we're live in 10 seconds ... 9 ... 8 ..." He counted the rest of the numbers down silently before giving Chase the go sign.

"Bwa-ha-ha-ha-ha! Hello again, listeners of the Murder Hour. This is your tailor of tells."

Rogers winced, hoping most listeners missed that slip.

"From the shores of Lake Superior to the dark streets of Minneapolis, we bring you tales of murder and mayhem, live from the KBGZ studios and brought to you by Magic Biscuits, the just-add-water biscuit that tastes like it was made from scratch!

At least he got the sponsor right, Rogers thought.

"Tonight our story takes us to an average street, just like in your neighborhood, where we find an average man, just like the one who lives next door ..."

The rest of the broadcast went off almost flawlessly, with only a few stumbles by the inexperienced star-for-the-day. All told, Rogers thought, they had dodged a bullet. It turned out the kid wasn't that bad.

"Bwa-ha-ha-ha-ha! Hello again, this is your teller of tales on The Murder Hour. *Poor Johnny. I guess he learned that murder is a losing business. Killers always end up ... in the red.*

"And don't forget to join us at 7 p.m. next Sunday for the next episode of The Murder Hour, *live from the KBGZ studios."*

Rogers let out a long breath as he signaled all clear to the cast. His shirt was almost completely soaked and sweat was covering his forehead. He grabbed the towel he had been using to wipe his face during the show, then threw it down again when he realized it was already sopping wet. He started to collapse into his chair when he heard the door of the studio slam open.

He looked up to see two Brickton police officers and a graying, thin man whose well-worn brown suit could only mean he was a detective. The police detective was waving a piece of paper as he entered.

"Keith Rogers, you're coming with us. You're under arrest for the murder of Kent Franklin."

IV

BLAKE RANDOLPH was pacing the floor in the lobby of the Brickton Police Department. It had been nearly two hours since Rogers was arrested and the publisher was getting short on patience.

"Sergeant," he said, again approaching the desk. "Your officers stormed into my radio station almost two hours ago and arrested one of my employees and I'd like to know what's going on. Mr. Lincoln here," he said, gesturing to the small seating area where a dignified, white-haired man waited, "is an attorney and he would like to see his client."

Sgt. Nelson sighed, restraining his annoyance. He knew that losing his temper with one of the most influential men in Minnesota was not going to serve him well.

"Yes, sir, Mr. Randolph. I have nothing new for you. The chief was out at Coney Island for the weekend, and he's on his way here right now," he said, referring to the resort island in Lake Waconia. "Until then, we've been told to ask you to wait for him. Sir."

Blake attempted to stay calm. "I understand you are just doing your job, Sergeant, and I'm not trying to throw my weight around. I just want to make sure my friend's rights are being observed."

"Sir, I can assure you he is being treated with the respect he deserves," Sgt. Franklin said with a straight face.

"Of course," Blake said with a grimace. "Why would I expect any different?"

He returned to the small group of uncomfortable chairs in the lobby, but within minutes resumed his pacing. It was another 30 minutes before the door opened and the recently appointed police chief walked in.

Chief Scott Morgan was a newcomer to Brickton. The city council, in an effort to erase some unfortunate incidents from the department's past, had brought Morgan in only a few months ago from Elk Ridge, Indiana, where he had been the police chief of that rural community. The belief was that an outsider would be able to bring a new perspective. Randolph, as the Red Jackal, had had a role in the previous chief's early retirement. Many in the city hadn't decided yet if the new chief was in over his head, but to all appearances, he was an honest man.

"Mr. Randolph," he said nodding in his direction. "Mr. Lincoln."

Lincoln jumped up with an agility that belied his age and quickly approached the chief, who towered over the attorney. Grant Abraham Lincoln may have shared a name with the former president, but barely cleared five feet in height.

"Chief Morgan, my client is being held somewhere in this station, we think, but we have as yet been unable to see him," Lincoln said. "I'm sure I don't have to tell you of the state of Minnesota's laws on right to counsel. The state Supreme Court has been very clear on this issue — "

The chief held out his hands as he attempted to placate the lawyer, generally known as one of the best and most ferocious defense attorneys in the state.

"Counsellor, I just arrived, but if what you say is true, that's certainly a problem. Sgt. Nelson," he said turning toward the desk. "Where is Mr. Rogers right now?"

The sergeant's pale, freckled skin flushed, as he looked uncomfortably at the chief. "Uh, sir," he said, barely speaking above a whisper. "Detective Deppler said to wait before letting anyone in, and, uh … they've got him in the interview room …"

The chief let out an exasperated sigh. "Go get Deppler."

Nelson scurried off, while Morgan stepped behind the front counter. Nelson returned with Deppler in less than 60 seconds. While Blake and the attorney couldn't hear the words, Morgan's angry gestures and Deppler's expression made it easy to interpret most of the conversation. Detective Louis Deppler was one of the old guard in the department and had been considered to be the top internal candidate when the previous chief retired. The scuttlebutt was that he had little respect for the new chief and that the feeling was mutual.

"Now!" Blake heard the chief say before Deppler stormed off. The chief quickly strode back to the two waiting men.

"Mr. Lincoln, let's go see your client."

Lincoln didn't look happy when he emerged an hour later from behind the half-wall separating the lobby from the rest of the station. When Blake started to head out the side door, he made a "follow me" gesture to Blake before walking out the front door of the station.

They stepped outside to find several reporters standing on the station steps, including Jennifer Jones of the *Gazette*.

"What's going on, chief? All we've heard is that Keith Rogers was arrested for murdering Kent Franklin!" she said.

Lincoln jumped in before Blake could say anything. "Mr. Rogers is innocent. We have no doubt that the Brickton Police Department has made a terrible mistake and arrested the wrong man. We certainly regret the death of such an esteemed member of the community as Mr. Franklin, but rest assured Mr. Rogers is innocent of any crime."

The gathered horde of journalists started shouting questions at the two men. "Is it true you're paying for his defense?" "Why did the police arrest him?" "Does this have anything to do with the fight Saturday?"

"We have nothing else to say at this time," Lincoln said, grabbing Blake's arm to pull him through the crowd. He stayed silent as they made the quick walk across City Square Park to his law office.

"We could have gone out the back, but I wanted to feed those newshounds something for the morning editions, even if it's just a note of innocence," Lincoln said as they stepped through the door of his office.

Lincoln gestured for Blake to walk into the inner office, striding past where his secretary would have been during normal business hours.

Blake shook his head and smiled slightly as they walked in. It never failed to amuse him that despite Lincoln's success, he continued to work in the same two-room office he had for the last 30 years. The worn leather chairs and scratched and dented oak desk gave the impression of a lawyer struggling to get by, not one of the richest men in the Twin Cities.

"I take it from the expression on your face that you're not quite as convinced of Keith's innocence as you proclaimed to the fourth estate?" he said as he sat down.

"Quite the opposite, actually," Lincoln replied. "Three decades of defending criminals has given me a pretty good sense for when someone is feeding me a load of malarkey. My conversation with Mr. Rogers has me convinced he's innocent. That, unfortunately, does not equal the same thing as not guilty in a court of law or the court of public opinion, my friend. Speaking of which, what is the *Gazette's* role going to be in this?"

"I already talked to Rod Stanley. Since I'm footing the bill for the defense, I want to be kept totally out of the loop on our coverage. The newsroom needs to run with whatever they have.

My personal feelings aren't important.

"Now, if you think he's innocent, what's the problem?"

"I haven't gotten a look at everything yet, but they're saying it's a convincing case. It seems Kent Franklin was shot in his apartment very early this morning. The murder weapon was a Colt .45 – an old pistol from the Great War – just like Rogers owned."

"Hold on a minute, there are thousands of those around. I still have one."

"Before I got in there he told them exactly where his Colt was – on the top shelf of his bedroom closet – but the police said they couldn't find it … and they said they could identify the one they found in Franklin's room as his, but I'm not sure how."

"So they're saying he just killed Kent, left his gun behind and went home?"

"Yeah, they were pretty circumspect about that. Deppler said the way Franklin was killed proved it was Keith. Add to that the fact that half the city heard about their fight at the Chestnut Grille, and, well, they were looking at him as soon as they found Franklin's body this morning."

"What does Keith say?"

"Well, that he didn't do it, but he doesn't know where his gun is, and he says he went home after dinner with Margaret O' Malley at the Grille. Sleeping alone in bed doesn't offer much of an alibi."

Blake stood up. "Whatever you need to spend, spend it. Whatever it costs, we're going to prove Keith is innocent."

V

THE TRUTH was the night was far from over for the Red Jackal.

After saying his goodnights to Lincoln, Blake returned to the *Gazette* building. He entered through the back employee entrance to avoid drawing attention, strode through the empty lobby and took the elevator up to the broadcasting studios that capped the building.

A quick glance as he stepped off the elevator confirmed that the floor was deserted. With the station concluding its broadcast day at 9 p.m., he had expected nothing else. While his presence could be easily explained – he did, after all, own the building – he preferred to be unseen as he verified something he had noticed the previous week.

He moved quietly to Keith Rogers' office and quickly began opening and closing drawers on the battered metal desk. He found the item for which he was looking in the back of the small bottom drawer. He removed the small box and opened the case to verify what he had suspected.

"Oh, Keith, you old-fashioned gentleman," he said with a smile.

Blake returned the box to where he had found it. After ensuring that everything else in the studio was as it had been when he arrived, he took the elevator to the building's basement. The basement, used strictly for storage, was empty in the post-midnight hours, although Blake could hear the hum of the printing presses one floor above him as they finished their run of the final edition. He made his way through the labyrinth of shelves, crates and discarded equipment. Even in the dim light, Blake could quickly find his path through the meandering mess.

He paused when he reached the dark, musty, far back corner of the basement, using his superior hearing to make sure no one else was in the basement. He moved over to where an

unmarked manhole cover led to the sub-basement. Most people who worked for the *Gazette* didn't even know the building had a sub-basement and the plans on file at city hall made no mention of it. Those who did know it existed had no interest in visiting it due to the constant flooding from the nearby Minnesota River.

He easily lifted the 250-pound cover to reveal a passage that dropped down about 10 feet into a flooded tunnel where there appeared to be at least three feet of standing water. Looking and listening one more time, he reached for an oddly placed light switch mounted on a nearby steel pole. A flick of the switch created a barely audible whirring sound and the water level quickly dropped as the pumps did their work. The tunnel was dry within two minutes and Blake climbed down to the floor of the tunnel, pulling the manhole closed behind himself.

The shaft was about six feet wide at floor level, appearing to be made of a run of yellow Brickton brick broken by only a steel door. But in reality the brick was only a façade over the steel walls that kept the space water tight. Blake opened the steel door to reveal a well-lit – and completely dry – brick tunnel. Despite expectations, a system of pumps and waterproofing ensured the tunnel stayed dry even when the Minnesota River ran over its banks in the spring. A line of rails ran into the distance and what appeared to be a silver miniature single-seat subway car sat 10 feet away.

Only a handful of people knew the brick tunnels existed. Blake had built the system of underground tunnels – with the assistance of some powerful friends – over the last decade as a way of quickly making his way around the city unobserved.

Blake securely closed the steel door, which on this side resembled the door of a submarine, cranking it shut. A flick of another switch reversed the pumps and water could be heard running back into the shaft, re-flooding it, preserving the illusion.

He slid into the car, which his brother David had dubbed the Zeppelin, and shoved the throttle forward. The Zeppelin sprang forward, the lights in the tunnel blurring as it swiftly increased speed, hurtling toward the Randolph family home.

The Zeppelin delivered Blake to the basement of his home in a matter of minutes. He only stayed at the house long enough to change into his guise as the Red Jackal. Putting on his scarlet suit, cape and cowl, he was recognizable to the lower elements as the vigilante crimefighter.

Those in power in the Twin Cities knew the Red Jackal only as a rumor. But those who made their living on the street, in both honest and dishonest endeavors, knew the truth behind the tales of the Red Jackal.

While the Jackal could have awakened Geoffrey – his driver, attaché and all-around Man Friday – he didn't expect to need the British secret service veteran tonight. Instead, he opted to drive the black armored Packard himself to the bungalow on the edge of Brickton's small downtown. When he pulled silently to the curb half a block away, he was surprised to see a light on in the small house, as he knew the occupant was otherwise occupied.

The Jackal didn't expect that the small Brickton police department would put one of their few men on duty watching the house. On the off chance that they were, though, he took a roundabout approach to the home. He quietly jogged down a side street, slipping into the alley running behind the homes, passing several dark garages and empty cars. When he arrived behind 320 Walnut St., he ascertained that he was still alone in the alley before approaching the rear of the home. From the alley he could see a red-haired woman rummaging through a dresser in the bungalow's lone bedroom, the room lit only by a small table lamp.

He moved to the rear door and found it, unsurprisingly, unlocked. He slipped silently into the main room of the home. To his right was the small kitchen; to his left the bedroom where he had seen the intruder. As he stealthily approached the rear bedroom, he could hear the loud sounds of a frantic search mixed with sobs.

"Hello, Miss O'Malley," the Jackal said as he entered the room.

Keith Rogers's secretary let out a quick scream as she spun around. She gasped as she saw the Jackal, then picked up an ashtray from the dresser and hurled it at him. He easily ducked the projectile and just as easily grabbed the secretary as she attempted to run past him.

"Let me go!" she said as she tried to wriggle out of his iron grip. "Let go!"

"Miss O'Malley, I believe we are on the same side here."

She stopped struggling to look at him, really noticing his appearance for the first time.

"You ... you're ... the Red Jackal ..."

"Yes, Miss O'Malley, and I'm here to help Mr. Rogers. I believe he's innocent and I imagine you know he is."

Her eyes widened at that.

"Why do you ..." she trailed off, then started to cry again.

He let go of her arms and guided her to the sofa, taking the chair across from her.

"I have no desire to keep you here against your will, but finding you in Mr. Rogers' home has been a serendipitous occurrence. Can I count on you to give me just a few minutes?"

Margaret O'Malley nodded, sniffling as she tried to hold back the tears.

"As I said, I believe that Mr. Rogers is innocent of these charges."

"Of course he is! Keith would never hurt anyone – especially not an arrogant blowhard like Kent Franklin!"

The Jackal leaned forward in his chair, looking her in the eyes.

"So what were you doing here tonight, Miss O'Malley?"

"I was trying to … find something."

The Jackal nodded. "I could see that. What were you looking for?"

"I'm not sure I should …"

"I believe in being direct, Miss O' Malley, so let me just ask you this: how long have you and Mr. Rogers been married?"

As she gasped and stared at him dumbfounded, the Jackal knew his supposition had hit the mark.

"But how did you …"

"Some observation and a couple of other facts I learned tonight, but I am curious why the secrecy?"

She buried her face in her hands then looked at him.

"We got married two months ago, but haven't told my parents yet. You see, I'm Catholic and Keith is Jewish. I can't imagine what their reaction would be if I wired them that I was married and my new husband was Jewish. But I'm supposed to be visiting them back in Michigan next month and Keith is going to come with me … and, well, we hope that if we tell them in person, they'll accept it.

"We've hidden it because my mother's cousin, Jeanette, works at the *Gazette* – she's the one who got me the job – and we didn't want my parents to find out from her.

"But we love each other so much … we just couldn't wait. And if my parents still have a problem after they meet Keith, then we'll come back here and that's that. But at least we can try."

She took a deep breath. "That's what I was looking for in the dresser – Keith's wedding ring. It might seem silly, but when we're here in private we wear them. He keeps his in the dresser and I couldn't find it. I keep mine here," she said, pulling the chain out from her dress to show a diamond ring.

The Jackal shook his dead disgustedly. "It wouldn't be the first time that jewelry disappeared from a suspect's house, but we have more important things to worry about right now. Most importantly, I think you can prove Rogers is innocent."

"What?"

"I have a source inside the police department," he started, bending the truth slightly. "Franklin was killed late Saturday night. Mr. Rogers insisted he was alone after 9 p.m. that night. To put it bluntly, Miss O'Malley, I assume that is a lie and you were with him?"

"Yes, yes, we were here …"

"I can only assume he is trying to protect your reputation. Telling the police a presumably single woman had spent the night with him … well, everything I know about your husband tells me he is a gentleman."

"I'll go to the police tomorrow and tell them everything!"

"Let's wait on that. Even disregarding the potential for scandal, there's a good chance they wouldn't believe you. A wife covering for her husband isn't unheard of in criminal cases. There are a lot of other problems with their case and your testimony may not be necessary to prove your husband's innocence."

Recognizing that it wasn't a good idea to stay in the Rogers home for much longer, the Jackal recommended that Margaret return to her apartment while he searched the home for evidence that might help in the case. After she left through the back door, he spent 20 minutes examining the small home, but found nothing that would help prove the director's innocence.

Still, there was one happy development. Buried beneath a pile of socks in a dresser drawer, he found the wedding ring. *At least I can deliver that good news tomorrow*, he thought.

VI

THE NEXT two days produced no new information in the case. By late Tuesday, Blake Randolph was feeling increasingly frustrated. He had still not been able to speak to Rogers directly; even the Red Jackal couldn't easily break into a jail.

Lincoln had met again with the jailed man but had learned little new. Blake hadn't told him yet of Margaret O'Malley's revelation, knowing the lawyer would want to know how he had come about the information. He intended to protect the lovers' secret – and the Red Jackal's – as long as he could.

He had put the Red Jackal to work again the previous night, but at this point his efforts had been nothing more than random questioning of his usual sources. Unsurprisingly, that had failed to shake anything loose; this didn't feel like the type of crime that would be solved by working the streets.

He was pondering another evening of fruitless searching when Jennifer Jones marched into his office.

"Chief, you have to see this," she said, handing him a page of copy.

"Whoa," he said when he saw the headline, throwing it back in her direction as if the page was on fire. "I made it clear I didn't want to know about our reporting on the murder!"

Jennifer signed theatrically, before pushing it back across his desk.

"Calm down. This is my finished article. You'd be able to see it in a couple hours when you approved the early edition. I just sent it down to the typesetters and unless something new comes in soon, I'm not making any changes."

She pointed at the page before sitting down in the chair opposite his. "Check out the third paragraph."

He skipped down the page and started reading.

Chief Morgan said Tuesday that officers questioned Rogers after hearing word of an altercation between him and Franklin Saturday night at the Chestnut Grille. However, according to a source in the Brickton Police Department, police also have another reason to suspect the radio director and writer, a detail shared exclusively with the Gazette.

While it is public knowledge that the actor was shot early Sunday morning, a police source said late Tuesday that he was actually killed by a complicated contraption rigged to a lamp in his westside apartment. As far as investigators have been able to determine a gun was mounted on the lamp, designed to fire when the pull string on the lamp was used to turn it on.

This particularly interested investigators as it is the exact same method used to kill a millionaire recluse in the second episode of The Murder Hour, *the new radio show from KBGZ radio in Brickton. Keith Rogers created the series and writes every episode, including that one.*

The Brickton Police Department refused to comment on the report, citing the ongoing investigation.

In other developments Tuesday …

"How did you … wait, never mind. I don't want to know. Are you sure about this?"

"I went over everything with Rod," she said, referring to the paper's city editor. "I've got two sources confirming it and from the look on the chief's face when I cornered him this afternoon, it's true."

Blake slammed both hands down on his desk.

"That's ridiculous. No, not your story," he said as he saw the look of dismay on Jennifer's face. "The theory. How stupid would Keith have to be to kill someone using his own method? I mean that is just idiotic. This has got Deppler written all over it. What's the idea? He just thought no one would notice he had written about his murder method? This literally makes no sense. Does anybody else have it?"

"I don't think so. Jacobi from the *Star* has been hanging around the courthouse all day, but he's new to the crime beat. They don't trust him yet. Besides, I've got better legs," she added with a mischievous grin.

"Not funny, Jones," Blake said. "Keep working on it – but I still don't want to see anything that isn't getting printed."

"You've got it, chief," Jennifer said with a quick salute as she left the office.

The problem, Blake realized, was that as much as this cleared Keith in his mind, the police department's theory of the crime had just blown Keith's alibi out of the water. If Franklin had really been killed by some sort of self-activated murder contraption, then it wouldn't matter one bit that Margaret O'Malley and Keith Rogers had spent the night together.

"NOOOO!!!"

The killer tipped over his kitchen table, sending coffee, eggs and toast flying across the room.

"NO!!!" he yelled again, picking up that morning's *Gazette*, then throwing it back to the floor. He took a deep breath and calmed himself.

Idiots. The world is nothing but idiots. He had clearly laid out the pattern for them. He *wanted* them to see the pattern. They had tied the Franklin murder to *The Murder Hour*, but missed the other two. Three murders, three matching radio episodes.

The article had suggested it might be an attempt to frame

Keith Rogers. If he had wanted to frame Rogers, he wouldn't have been that clumsy about it. He had clearly given the world too much credit. If they couldn't see the pattern he would show them.

He fell to his knees and prayed to a God he didn't necessarily believe in, but still feared.

Blake parked the green Packard – the unarmored, non-bullet proof, factory-issue one – in his reserved spot behind the *Gazette* building Wednesday morning and stepped out of the front door into the oppressive humidity of the July morning. *Anyone who thinks of Minnesota as a frigid wasteland needs to be here in the summer*, he though as he felt the moisture assault him. *Ten o'clock in the morning and it's already miserable.*

What he wouldn't give to be at the family's cabin on Lake Ludlow. His brother David was up there now on an extended fishing trip. Blake had just spent the 4th of July weekend there, but he was ready to go back.

"Blake!"

He turned to see Lincoln, clad in a white suit, jogging his way, as reality intruded on his daydreams. Blake stopped walking across the parking lot and waited for the lawyer to catch him. Lincoln put his hands on his knees and paused to catch his breath when he caught up with Blake.

"I'm getting … too old to move like that," he said, coughing once.

"Sorry," he said, straightening up. "I wanted to get you before you got inside."

"Why? What's wrong?"

"Nothing's wrong! That lady reporter of yours has got the police running around like the Keystone Kops. They're all trying to figure out who talked and forming their own little circular firing squad. Quite amusing, actually!

"But that's not actually what I needed to talk to you about. We have another hearing tomorrow afternoon with Judge Preston to revisit the bail question. I thought you might want to be there. I also think I might be able to get you in to see Keith after the hearing, assuming he doesn't get out."

"Great. Is he going to get bail?" Blake asked as he wiped the sweat from his forehead.

"Hard to say. Judge Preston can be tough, but he's fair. If he does get bail, it's likely to be pretty high, probably more than Keith can afford ..."

"Don't worry about that, Grant. I'll take care of it."

"Alright, Blake," Lincoln said as the men shook hands. "I'll be in touch."

As the attorney turned back toward his office, Blake headed for the back door of the Gazette building, feeling his suit already clinging to his body. *What a miserable day*, he thought as he entered the building.

He took the elevator to the third-floor newsroom. It took him more than 10 minutes to make it all the way to his office as he engaged in several conversations about the ongoing murder story and other topics.

"Good morning, Kate," he said as he walked past his long-time assistant's office.

"Good morning, Blake," she responded. "The mail is on your desk. Nothing that looks too important."

"Great, thanks," he said as he hung up his jacket on the hook behind his door and walked over to the desk. As promised, a large stack of mail sat on the corner of his desk. He groaned inwardly as looked at the pile. *That can wait.*

As he stepped behind his desk, he saw an envelope resting on his chair, "Blake Randolph – Personal & Private" written on it.

"Kate?" He held up the envelope as she stuck her head in the door. "What's this? It was on my chair."

She moved over to the desk to take a closer look. "I don't know. There's no stamp, so it's not part of the regular mail. I suppose someone could have dropped it off. I've been away from my desk several times this morning and …"

"And my open-door policy that you have frequently complained about makes it easy for anyone who wants to to come into my office?"

"To put it bluntly, yes," she replied, not unkindly. "I don't mean to point out the obvious, but perhaps you should open it?"

"That *was* going to be my next move."

He opened the envelope, removing a single sheet of paper. He quickly read the text, then looked back at Kate.

"Call Chief Morgan. Now."

VII

Dear Mr. Randolph:

I read with dismay the article in the Gazette *yesterday. As a loyal subscriber, I was disappointed to see such a misunderstanding of the murder of Kent Franklin. While I am not surprised the Brickton Police Department failed to solve the crime, it is unfortunate that your reporter has not unearthed the full importance of the information included in her article.*

I feel it is necessary for me to give both you and the police additional help in solving the murder of Mr. Franklin. The supposition that the murder was inspired by The Murder Hour *is quite correct. Unfortunately, everyone has failed to see the larger pattern. This was the third murder inspired by that fine radio program.*

I suppose it's important I explain how I know this. To state it concisely, I am the one responsible. I have enjoyed The Murder Hour *since its debut earlier this year, especially the ingenious ways criminals have been dispatched.*

I expect that both you and the police department will be inclined to dismiss this as the rambling of some deranged person, so allow me to detail the deaths. First of all, of course, we have Kent Franklin, who was killed in the same method as Mr. McCartney in the second episode of the series. It took quite a bit of experimenting to get that to work.

But as I said, that was actually the third killing. As our little show takes place throughout the state, it only seemed fitting that the real-life version do so as well. With that in mind, you can find the first death in Duluth: the unidentified body found in the Forest Park Cemetery – strangled to death in a cemetery just like our poor criminal Frankie in the July 3 episode. By the way, the young man was a deckhand on a ship that had just docked in the harbor. Let's just say he was looking for a service I had no interest in providing, but it made an easy way to draw him away. Perhaps you can check with some of the shipping companies to find out his identity.

The second death was a little closer to home. This one took a little more work as I had to find someone alone in a tall building late at night. Luckily, there's almost always someone working late on the weekends. Police dismissed his death as a suicide (understandable when one reads about his life … he really was a miserable individual), but Mr. Bertrand James was helped out the window on the 12th floor of the Armstrong Tower. This death was, of course, inspired by the murder of our blackmailer in the third episode.

To reiterate, Keith Rogers had no role in these killings, except, perhaps, as an inspiration. So let me be clear: The man is innocent and should be released from jail. The level of planning required for this piece of art is beyond a radio hack.

I know that you have received this letter and I fully expect it to be shared with the police department. I also fully expect them to do the right thing and release an innocent man from jail. I have no desire to see an innocent man suffer for a crime he did not commit. I eagerly await the news of his release.

Sincerely,
A loyal reader and listener
P.S. I imagine you might be tempted to stop broadcasting The

Murder Hour *from your station. That would be a very bad idea.*

"This doesn't prove anything," Deppler said as he finished reading the letter. Deppler and Chief Morgan had arrived at the *Gazette* office minutes after Kate's call. Blake had been unhappy to see the detective enter with the chief.

"I'm afraid I have to agree with my detective, Blake," said the chief, who had read the letter before sharing it with Deppler. "There's no way to prove that the letter writer is telling the truth. Both of those deaths made the papers. Heck, I read about both of them myself in the *Gazette*. It would be easy enough to create a story around them that makes Mr. Rogers look innocent."

Blake looked at both men, disbelief reflected on his face. "You can't be serious! Why would someone make something like this up? And in such detail?"

"Maybe to get a friend out of jail?" Deppler said. "I find it pretty convenient that this letter shows up in your office, with nobody seeing who delivered it. I wouldn't be surprised if —"

"Stop right there, Deppler," the chief warned. "We're not accusing you of anything, Blake. Most likely, this is the work of some nut who wants attention. This kind of thing happens all the time when there's a high-profile murder. Now, if more evidence develops, we can talk, but for now, we are following Judge Preston's instructions and Rogers will be arraigned tomorrow morning on murder charges.

"We will, of course, provide a copy of this letter to Mr. Lincoln and he can present it as evidence to the judge. As far as I'm concerned, it's up to him now. Now, we'd like to talk to your assistant about this to see if she can add anything."

"Go ahead. She's waiting for you at her desk," Blake said through gritted teeth, gesturing out the door.

As soon as they left, he picked up the phone to call Lincoln.

"No dice," Lincoln said. "Preston didn't see the need to release Keith. He said if the state's attorney wants to go ahead with the prosecution, the letter wasn't enough to release him."

It was nearing 3 p.m. as Lincoln and Blake sat in the publisher's office. At Lincoln's request, an emergency hearing had been held that afternoon to discuss the letter. Blake hadn't been able to attend due to a meeting in Minneapolis with federal regulators as he sought to obtain the permits to increase the strength of the radio station.

In front of a packed courtroom, Lincoln had asked the judge to release Keith Rogers immediately in light of the new evidence. The state's attorney had argued that it was, on its own, not enough to overshadow the rest of the evidence. The judge had agreed, but said he would consider letting the letter be used as evidence.

"It's a partial victory, at least," Lincoln said. "I hadn't really expected to get the whole case tossed today, but it was worth trying. If nothing else, it helps us with the potential jury pool. I saw plenty of reporters there."

Blake picked up the copy of the letter on his desk, sighed and put it back down.

"What do you make of this, Grant?"

"I think it's legitimate, but it's different than most cases I've dealt with. Most crimes are simple at their heart, crimes of passion or opportunity. People kill or steal because of jealousy or to enrich themselves," he said. "You've been involved in plenty of cases yourself over the years. What's your take on it?"

"That you're right. This is something different. That letter was chilling; the killer was proud of what he had done and wanted us to know he was responsible. And I don't think he's done."

VII

Rogers hadn't been released. That was unfortunate. He had attended today's court hearing, just one of the many in the crowded courthouse.

He had a brief moment of fear when Jennifer Jones saw him and made a brief greeting. But he quickly calmed as he realized there was no reason he *shouldn't* be there. It seemed like half of Brickton was and, like many people in town, he had more than a passing acquaintance with the accused station manager.

What everyone seemed to fail to understand was that everyone he had killed had been guilty of crimes against man, against nature. When he said he had no desire to see an innocent man punished, he was telling the truth. He had been raised to be a moral person; to fear Hell and its punishments. He had his doubts about Heaven, but he was sure there was a Hell for those who didn't follow a moral code. In his own way, he was merely helping Satan claim his own … albeit a little early.

Still, it probably was stupid to be in the courtroom. The police chief and the detective were there and as incompetent as they were, they might just stumble on something. His bigger concern was someone like Jones putting two and two together. She had, after all, come closer to uncovering the truth than anyone else. He hoped that … well, never mind.

The real wildcard was the Red Jackal. Yes, like everyone else in Brickton, he had heard the rumors of the vigilante crimefighter. If the man – if he was a man – existed, it explained what happened to a lot of the criminals in town. The Red Jackal, he figured, had to have a secret identity with which he lived his everyday life. That meant he needed to be careful. No more satisfying his ego by showing up in court or sticking around at the crime scenes.

Unfortunately, it appeared that the police hadn't gotten the message yet. He never did like the slow students.

"That hick is going to screw this up and then he can go back to growing corn or whatever they do there in Indiana, as far as I'm concerned. That job should have been mine and everybody in the department knows it."

Brickton police officer Chris Landon looked around the Chestnut Grille, which was relatively empty on this Wednesday night.

"Keep it down, Deppler," he said in a loud whisper. "You don't need to get yourself fired."

"I don't care who hears me!" the intoxicated man said loudly.

That caused those few patrons that were in the restaurant to turn toward their table in the rear of the restaurant. Matt Sweeney, the restaurant's manager, also looked in their direction. "Landon ..." he said, not really wanting to have to toss anyone from the police department out of the Grille, no matter how obnoxious they were.

Landon acknowledged the warning with a nod before turning back to Deppler. "You said you wanted to talk, so I'm here. But even if you don't care about your job, I need mine. The Minneapolis department just let another dozen officers go. I lose this job and I'm moving back to *my* family's farm. And I've milked quite enough cows, thank you very much."

"Alright, alright. You're right. Sorry. I'm just tired of Morgan. Do you know he wanted to release Rogers today? If it was up to him, that murderer would be walking free today."

It was an old refrain from Deppler, one Landon, his best friend on the force, had heard ever since Morgan was hired that spring. When the previous police chief retired, everyone had assumed that Deppler would be the next leader of the department. After that failed to happen, Landon had spent the last six months watching a previously solid – if unspectacular – detective start cutting corners and making mistakes. Unfortunately, Morgan's arrival had coincided almost perfectly with the passage of the Cullen-Harrison Act. Deppler had taken good advantage of the availability of beer and wine again. The truth was at this point, Landon was practically the only one who would have anything to do with Deppler. And even he was losing patience with the detective.

"Louis. Listen to me. This constant griping isn't doing you any good. Look at it this way: if Morgan does screw up and get fired, you want to be the one the city turns to this time. That's not going to happen if you keep complaining. Seeming like a sore loser won't do you any good."

Deppler's mumbled response was drowned out by a sudden surge of people into the restaurant. The Chestnut Grille went from nearly empty to packed in what seemed like only a few moments. Landon glanced at his watch and realized that the 7 p.m. show at the adjacent Rex Theatre had just let out; he had heard that Barbara Stanwyck was really something in the flick.

"What?" he said, looking back at Deppler.

"Nothing. I'm going to get another drink."

He was up and out of his chair before Landon could respond, pushing his way through the crowd. He was back in less than five minutes, holding two Hamm's, but with a angry look on his face.

"What's wrong?" Landon asked, dreading the answer.

"Some idiot bumped into me with a fork or a pen or something. Look at this," he said, holding up his right arm and showing Landon a small puncture mark.

"I couldn't see who it was," he said to Landon's unasked question. "Somebody in that crowd of people from the Rex. I was at the bar and I felt it, but they were gone by the time I turned around. Just more crap."

Landon tried not to sigh too loudly at the latest woe-is-me complaint from Deppler.

"Hey," he said in an effort to change the subject. "So I heard that *Baby Face* is quite the movie. What do you say we take Jill and Katie to see it Saturday. From what I hear, it sets the quite the mood," he added with a wink.

"Yeah ... sure, that's a good ... a good ..."

Landon noticed that Deppler had turned pale, almost gray and his eyes were clouding over.

"Louis, you OK?"

"Yeah, I'm ... I'm fine. I think I just need some air. It's just getting too crowded in here." He pushed himself up from the table, then staggered back toward his chair. He took one step forward before pitching forward. His forehead hit the solid oak table with a loud crack as he bounced off the surface and onto the floor.

Landon leapt out of his seat and quickly felt for a pulse, finding none. "Someone get a doctor!" he yelled, knowing that it was almost certainly too late for anyone to help the detective.

"Chief, you better come look at this."

Chief Morgan walked slowly over toward the bar where his only surviving detective, Warren Pike, was holding up an envelope. Morgan had been at the Chestnut Grille for about 30 minutes. He and Pike had questioned Landon, who was sitting to the side of the now empty restaurant. He had shared the story of an evening with two friends grabbing dinner – and complaining about the chief, Morgan assumed.

He told of the events leading up to Deppler's collapse. Dr. Chester, a local physician, had been in the restaurant, but said Deppler was dead by the time he reached his side. The body had been taken to the Rand Funeral Home, with strict orders not to touch it until the medical examiner from Hennepin County could be tracked down and brought out to Brickton.

"It's addressed to you, sir. It was under this glass here," he said, indicating a glass full of beer sitting on the end of the bar. There had been a large amount of garbage strewn around as a lot of people cleared out pretty quickly when they realized what had happened. Morgan's officers were still trying to track down the patrons that had scattered to the winds.

He saw "Chief Morgan" in large block letters as he took the envelope from Pike. He opened the unsealed envelope and saw the typed letter he feared had been inside.

Dear Chief Morgan:

I'm assuming you will be on site yourself to receive this. By now, you probably suspect that Detective Deppler did not die of natural causes. That suspicion is quite correct.

I felt that after the failure to release Mr. Rogers, a further demonstration was needed of my sincerity in claiming responsibility for the earlier deaths. I'm sure you will discover the answer soon enough, but I will help you out by letting you know that the detective was poisoned with curare, delivered by a sharp pin.

I hope this proves, even to your doubting eyes, that I am the one and only person responsible for these deaths.

Although I suppose that's not really quite true. One of the characteristics of The Murder Hour *that I find particularly gratifying is that the murder victims always deserve their fate. They are criminals, blackmailers, evil people. Every person I have removed has been deserving of their fate as well. In the case of Deppler, it was for his failures as a detective, most notably accusing the innocent Mr. Rogers of murder and failing to recognize the true nature of the crime.*

Let his death be a warning of what happens to those who fail to pursue justice.

Signed, A Concerned Citizen

VIII

IT WAS nearly midnight by the time Chief Morgan arrived home. After parking his police cruiser in the garage he walked the 50 feet across the dark yard to the equally dark house.

The 44-year-old police chief lived alone; that was the way he wanted it. He had been married – in fact, had married his high school sweetheart in Elk Ridge. Louise's death two years ago from cancer had prompted him to search for somewhere, anywhere, else to live. After more than 20 years together, everything in Elk Ridge had reminded him of the love of his life.

Of course, it hadn't worked. All he did now was think about how much Louise would have liked the new house – and that she would be all over him to unpack all those boxes in the attic. But he wasn't thinking about any of that as he got home tonight.

Nor surprisingly, his thoughts were dominated by the murder of Deppler and the letter from the killer. Clearly, they had severely underestimated the man behind these killings. He had had his doubts about Rogers's guilt, but had deferred to Deppler in an attempt to appease the disgruntled detective. Little good it had done, though, and little it mattered now. The detective was a bastard who wanted to get rid of him, but he was still a cop.

The letter and its implications continued to run through his head as he made his way through the kitchen and into the front parlor on his way to the stairs to his upstairs bedroom. Without even knowing why, he drew his Smith & Wesson and spun as he passed his study, crouching into a shooting stance.

"I'm going to turn this lamp on, Chief Morgan," he heard a voice say from the darkness. "You can put that away."

"Go ahead, but if it's all the same to you, I'll keep this pointed in your direction."

The only response was a sudden flash as the burst of light from the lamp filled the room, revealing a man clad in scarlet suit and a scarlet hood with a small jackal insignia on it, sitting in a chair beside the chief's desk.

"You know, a time is going to come when you pull this little appearance act of yours and I'll end up shooting you," the chief said. "And it may not be an accident."

The Jackal chuckled. "Don't worry about that. You wouldn't be the first person to shoot at me. You wouldn't even be the first to hit me, for that matter. My recuperative powers are quite robust."

The Jackal spoke in the deep, gravelly voice he always used in the Jackal guise to hide his identity from those who knew Blake Randolph, as the police chief did. He noted that the chief had yet to lower his weapon, which was typical of his meetings with Brickton's top police officer. He had first visited the new chief only a few days after he started on the job, and had met with him several times over the ensuing months to offer his assistance. Those get togethers were frequently held at gunpoint.

Their partnership was a cautious one. Morgan appreciated his efforts to fight crime, but not his vigilante methods. He was still not entirely convinced the Jackal was completely on the side of good, but he had a hard time arguing with the results of his work.

"It's been a long night, Jackal. What do you want?"

"Yes, I heard about Detective Deppler. I can't say I approved of his methods, but I still am sorry to hear of his murder. More importantly, I'm here to talk about the letter from our killer."

"Now wait a minute … how did you … ?" the chief blurted out in exasperation. Only a handful of people knew about the letter, let alone its contents. "Never mind. I'm sure you'd just give me some cryptic response about the sands of Egypt or the power to cloud men's minds, or something like that. How about I just concede the point and we'll move on."

The Jackal smiled beneath his cowl. "The truth is, chief, that in this case the problem is that your department leaks like a sieve. I'd imagine the *Gazette*, the *Star*, the *Journal* and everyone with a police reporter already knows about it, or will soon."

Morgan grimaced, knowing it was probably true. "I don't suppose you're here to tell me who the killer is?"

"Unfortunately, no. But I think this latest letter gives us an opening. I have a plan on how to get him to reveal himself, but it's going to require your help. First of all, I need you to hold a press conference tomorrow ..."

After spending an hour convincing Chief Morgan to give his plan a shot ("It's either brilliant or the dumbest idea I've ever heard," the chief had said.) the Jackal had headed for home. On his way, he radioed Geoffrey to let him know the plan was a go. As always, despite the late hour, his invaluable jack-of-all-trades sounded wide awake and refreshed.

He arrived to find Geoffrey hard at work creating the devices he would need for the press conference. The Jackal quickly shed his costume and joined Geoffrey in the workshop deep beneath the Randolph estate.

"The press conference is at 2 p.m. on the courthouse steps," he said. "You'll have everything ready by then?"

"It won't be a problem, sir," the unflappable Brit responded. "Compared to some of your past requests, these devices will be quite simple to create. In fact, they should be ready for testing in about an hour."

Geoffrey beat his own estimate, in fact, having the necessary equipment completed in barely 30 minutes. They both passed the Jackal's tests with flying colors.

"Well, Geoffrey, the rest is in Chief Morgan's hands. Now, I think we both need to get some rest. Tomorrow could be a very long day for both of us."

IX

THERE WAS a large crowd outside the County Courthouse at 1:55 p.m. the next afternoon. As the Jackal had predicted, news of the letter had already made its way through most of the assembled press and would be widely reported in that evening's newspapers.

The story had spread beyond Minnesota and reporters from as far away as Chicago had joined the usual collection of Twin Cities journalists to hear what Chief Morgan had to say. Add to that the dozens of worried citizens who had turned out and the Brickton police had been forced to close multiple downtown streets to preserve the safety of the crowd.

The Jackal had told Morgan he would be watching from the roof of the *Gazette* building. Morgan briefly looked in that direction from his position at the top of the courthouse steps, but saw no sign of the vigilante. He knew that didn't mean anything, as the tallest building in Brickton offered plenty of places where the Jackal could see the proceedings without being spotted from the ground.

He still had his doubts about the Jackal's plan to lure the killer out with such a blatant display, but he was desperate to eliminate this threat to his new city. And, frankly, while he never would have done something this stupid while Louise was alive, he found himself increasingly more willing to risk his life in the years since her death.

Jennifer Jones was in the front row, directly in front of the rostrum from which Morgan would be speaking. KBGZ had provided a microphone and sound system, which she could see would be needed for the large crowd. She estimated there were well over a hundred people in the crowd, buzzing with anticipation.

The bells of St. Albert's Catholic Church chimed the two o'clock hour and she watched Morgan walk down to the rostrum that had been set up on the large landing halfway up the courthouse steps.

Clad in his full dress uniform, Morgan projected an image of calm authority. He pulled his folded notes out of his jacket pocket and put on his glasses before leaning toward the microphone.

"Good afternoon," he began. "I want to thank all of our press for coming today, as well as all the concerned citizens. I have a statement to make, and then I'll take your questions.

"Last night, one of our city's fine police officers, Detective Louis Deppler, was killed by a cowardly murderer who has decided to take it upon himself to deliver his own twisted brand of justice. I know many of you have heard about the letter this killer left at the site, as well as a letter he sent to the *Brickton Gazette* earlier this week.

"In these letters, this person claims responsibility for the murder of not only Detective Deppler, but also Kent Franklin and two other killings – one in Minneapolis and one in Duluth. We are working with the police in those cities to determine the veracity of these claims, but at this point we believe them to be true. The writer of these letters has provided information that leads us to that conclusion; information we are not yet ready to share as part of our investigation."

Morgan paused and looked at the gathered crowd. The low murmur when he had begun speaking had been replaced by almost total silence.

"This raises two important issues. First, based on this investigation, it is the opinion of the Brickton Police Department that Keith Rogers is innocent of any connection to the murders. While it is true that the murders have mimicked stories that Mr. Rogers has created for his radio show, he is not responsible for how a twisted mind has used those stories. This morning, I personally recommended to the state's attorney that all charges against Mr. Rogers be dropped and that he be released immediately. My understanding is that process has already been started.

"Secondly, I want to make clear to this killer that he will be brought to justice. The full resources of the Brickton Police Department and multiple other authorities are dedicated to tracking you down and making sure you are punished for these crimes.

"You may have thought to deter us by murdering one of our detectives. Let me be clear: You can threaten us; you can even kill one of our own; that will not keep us from tracking you down."

Jennifer Jones looked back up at Morgan while she continued to scrawl in her notebook, trying to get every word down. Morgan reached to adjust the microphone as he leaned closer in.

"Finally, I want to —"

Morgan froze, his hand on the microphone, his mouth open in a silent scream. The members of the crowd began yelling, with some moving closer to the steps and others trying to flee in the other direction as they realized something had gone horribly wrong.

In the flurry of bodies, someone hit Jennifer's notebook out of her hand. She bent down to pick it up and was knocked to the ground. She quickly picked herself up and looked to the steps where a group of police officers had gathered around Morgan, now laying on the ground. Others were pushing the reporters away from the scene. Black smoke was leaking from the lectern.

"Back up ... give me room," she heard a voice yell. "Give me room."

As the small group moved back, she recognized the speaker as Dr. Springfield. She had noticed the Hennepin County medical examiner standing with the group of officials before Morgan started speaking.

"He's breathing, but unconscious. Let's go. We need to move him now," Springfield said to the police detective kneeling next to Morgan. Jones recognized him as Lt. Brian McDaniels of the Minneapolis Police Department. It was odd that he was here, she thought, but perhaps he was working the case on the Minneapolis murder or had been brought in for crowd control.

McDaniels and Dr. Springfield picked up Morgan and quickly carried him to what she assumed was Springfield's waiting car. Both men jumped in the car and sped off as the crowd parted, leaving the gathered journalists scrambling to figure out what had happened.

Detective Pike, now the highest-ranking member of the department, was barking out orders, attempting to restore order. Jennifer Jones joined the horde of reporters shouting questions at the detective.

Having listened to recordings of all the episodes of *The Murder Hour*, though, Jones, knew exactly what she had just seen. Like the homicidal radio star in one of last month's episodes, Chief Morgan had been electrocuted by a rigged microphone.

X

WHAT WENT wrong? He should be dead!

He was no engineer, but he had studied the equipment carefully. That careful planning had allowed him to rig the gun that had killed Kent Franklin. The way he rewired that microphone was meant to send such a jolt of electricity through the police chief that he should have been killed instantly.

When the police chief announced his press conference, the set-up seemed so perfect. The ultimate final act of his script.

Instead, he had heard the doctor say he was still breathing. The chief had been rushed to Brickton Memorial Hospital. He had managed to get close to some of the reporters outside the hospital. Rumors were flying as an entire section of the hospital had been blocked off and apparently Morgan had yet to regain consciousness. There was a huge police presence and only the medical staff had been allowed to see him.

He thought about trying to sneak into the hospital and finishing the job, but quickly dismissed the idea as impractical. *If he survives, he's going to have plenty of protection.*

Where to go from here? He hated to leave the job undone. All the other killings had been so perfect. Perhaps he had accomplished enough; his original goal had certainly been accomplished. He just hadn't counted on how much he would enjoy the planning, the challenge of outsmarting the investigators.

The killing was secondary. It wasn't so much that he enjoyed it, he just felt no guilt for it. Throughout his life he had always thought of other people as merely supporting players in the drama that was his life. They were props – extraneous noise to be filtered out. He supposed there were some that would say that said more about him than the rest of the world, but then … who cares what those people thought?

There would be incredible attention on him now. Accomplishing another masterpiece would be difficult, but that would make it all the sweeter …

The light had been fading in the western sky when Keith Rogers was finally released from jail. With all of the excitement around the injured police chief, getting an accused murderer – even one most likely innocent – out of jail had not been a priority for the department.

Lincoln had been waiting for him when deputies brought him out of the holding area into the lobby. He had offered to take the newly freed man somewhere for a celebratory dinner, but Rogers begged off, saying he would rather just "go home, take a shower and get to sleep."

The Red Jackal was already waiting in the director's home when he stepped through the front door just a few minutes later. This time, though, he wasn't alone.

The 40-year-old appeared to have aged another decade while in jail, looking haggard and pale, with large bags under his eyes. But he smiled when he saw Margaret O'Malley waiting for him in the dimly lit living room.

"Margaret, you are a sight for sore eyes," he said, stepping toward her and embracing her. He grabbed her around the waist, and pulled her toward him in a tight embrace. She quickly pulled away after a brief kiss, though.

"Is something wrong?" he asked.

"Well, we're not exactly alone," she said, looking toward the back bedroom. "Uh, Mr. Jackal?"

Rogers followed her gaze and stepped protectively in front of his wife when he saw the tall man, dressed all in scarlet, emerge from the room. "Who are you? What are you doing here?"

"It's fine, Keith. He's on our side," Margaret said, grabbing his arm. "This is the Red Jackal."

"Wait … the what?"

"That's correct, Mr. Rogers," the Red Jackal said quietly. "I can only apologize that it took this long to get you out of jail. I am aware of your relationship with Miss O'Malley here … although I suppose that appellation is no longer accurate. I have no desire to intrude on your reunion, but I do need a favor."

Rogers leaned forward with his hands on his hips, the light reflecting off his balding pate, with a scowl on his face.

"A favor? I just spent four days in jail. And I'm sorry, just because some guy dresses up like The Shadow and shows up in my house doesn't mean I need to help him!"

"You're right. You don't owe me anything. But I hope you

will do the right thing and help me stop this killer."

Rogers looked at Margaret and at the Jackal, then back to Margaret, and sighed. "OK, what do you need?"

"I now know who the real killer is, thanks to the attack on Chief Morgan this afternoon. I just need to prove it … and that's where I need your help. Both of you, in fact. I've already talked to Miss O'Malley about it. Tomorrow night you're going to record a special episode of *The Murder Hour*. You just need to convince your Mr. Randolph that it's a good idea."

"Are you insane?" Rogers exploded. "We've got a man obsessed with my show running around killing people and you want us to make another episode? What if he snaps and does something crazy?"

This time, the Jackal smiled, an expression that was more chilling than reassuring. "Actually, Mr. Rogers, that's exactly what I am hoping will happen."

XI

INTERESTING. SO The Murder Hour *is not going to broadcast live this week.*

He wasn't sure about the change in routine. Could it be an effort to affect his plans, to try and catch him? Was it possible someone knew who he was? Perhaps Keith Rogers had figured it out … or Blake Randolph? When the station owner and the director had made the announcement that afternoon, it had seemed reasonable enough. They had asked all of the employees in the building to come to the *Gazette* newsroom at noon … did they know he was there listening to them?

Randolph had explained why he gathered all of the employees together.

"This series of murders has put us in a situation where we're really not sure what to do next. As most of you know, the killer has threatened

more trouble if we stop running the show. Mr. Rogers came to me today with a plan that I think makes a lot of sense. He has written a script for this week that, well, I won't go into the details, but he believes will be difficult for the killer to replicate. In light of the killer's threats, we are going forward with our broadcast this week, but will be recording the show ahead of time. The police department has agreed to this plan and we have provided the script to them so they can prepare for anyone who does try to act on it.

"But here is why we have asked all of you here this afternoon. The team will be producing the script with only two actors and Keith handling the technical side of things ... just in case. I'm also sending everyone home by 5 p.m. today. I want this building empty when the recording begins at 8 o'clock tonight. The building will be locked and checked by the Brickton police before the cast starts working. There will be officers stationed in the lobby with Hank. This applies to me as well. This is for everyone's safety."

He had already gotten his hands on the script. Frankly, he thought it was weak ... nowhere near the quality Rogers had produced before. It was disappointing to see the show have such a pedestrian script. In all fairness, that was probably his fault.

He was still working on his plans for his finale ... he wasn't ready to act yet, still looking for a fitting denouement, still trying to find the right target. But perhaps ... *yes, Blake Randolph could be a fine substitute.* Things had gotten messy with the police chief, but a simple, straight-forward final act could tie everything up nicely ...

By 7:30 that night, the building had been checked and found empty ... even the *Gazette* newsroom. It wasn't widely known outside newsrooms, but most Saturday newspapers were put to bed early so the staff didn't have to work on Friday nights. While

usually a single reporter would be on duty to be ready for any late-breaking news, even that role had been abandoned for the evening.

Anyone who looked around the newsroom would see it in a state of silence and stillness rarely observed. So there was nobody there to observe that night as the photo darkroom slowly opened, the creaking of the door echoing across the empty newsroom.

Jennifer Jones winced at the sound, freezing in place and listening for any response. Hearing none, she slipped out from behind the door, then carefully closed it before looking around the darkened floor. As she had expected – or at least hoped – the officer who checked the newsroom had only opened the door to the darkroom and hadn't bothered looking in the small storage cabinet in the back corner. It had cost her a nice skirt, though, she thought as she looked with dismay at the brown stain from the developer she had spilled on herself squeezing into the closet.

If there's going to be a story here tonight, I'll be damned if I'm going to miss it, she thought as she headed across the newsroom to the stairs to make her way up to the sixth floor.

Keith Rogers double-checked the time: 7:58 p.m. They would start recording in just two minutes. The Jackal had made it clear he wanted the show to start promptly at 8 p.m. Rogers was directing and running the studio himself tonight. The script called for only two major roles and no sound effects. Only Harrison Chase – to play the narrator and major male role – and Margaret O'Malley – to handle the small female role in the middle act "flashback" – were joining him in the studio. The Red Jackal said he would be nearby, but Rogers had seen no sign of the vigilante.

Chase was alone in the booth for the first segment while

Margaret was joining Keith at the controls. She reached out and muted the network feed that was going out over the air. Then, knowing that Chase couldn't see him at the control panel from the brightly lit glass booth, Rogers pressed the intercom button and counted him down to the beginning of the recording. It was a departure from the usual procedure, but they had gone over the change earlier that evening.

"And give me a two count, Harrison, then go."

"Bwa-ha-ha-ha-ha! Hello again, listeners of the Murder Hour. This is your teller of tales.

"From the shores of Lake Superior to the dark streets of Minneapolis, we bring you tales of murder and mayhem, transcribed in the KBGZ studios and brought to you by Magic Biscuits, the just-add-water biscuit that tastes like it was made from scratch!

"Tonight's story finds us in Stillwater, where we'll join a guilty man pondering his fate as he waits for death. For while the state might not be able to kill him, that doesn't mean sentence still won't be carried out ... from beyond the grave ..."

As far as Rogers could tell, all was going according to plan ... not that he knew what that plan was. Even last night, the Jackal had been reticent when divulging the details.

"I think it's best if you don't know what is going to happen, but rest assured I will be in place to ensure you are both safe. The lights will go out during the first act – by my doing. When that happens, follow my instructions exactly."

The couple looked at each other, both waiting for the power outage. They were only half listening to Chase, knowing the recording would be unusable, that tonight's recording was simply a trap to lure the killer to the station. That's the part that Rogers didn't quite understand ... what was going to make the killer come here? As that thought flitted through his mind, he looked at the booth where Chase was reading the script, tilting his head in thought. Could it be ...

Before he could finish that thought, the studio plunged into darkness, causing Margaret to let out a short scream.

"Do not panic." The voice they recognized as the Red Jackal came from behind them. "Take this," he said, pushing a flashlight into Rogers's hands. "Go directly to the elevator and take it to the lobby."

"Wait," Rogers started. "Is Harrison ...?"

"Go. *NOW!*" The Jackal grabbed the two, each with one powerful arm and almost threw them toward the elevator bank.

The Jackal grabbed the microphone – which was still fully powered – and addressed the booth. Due to his enhanced hearing, he knew that the door had not opened and Chase was still there, probably worried about trying to move in the dark.

"Good evening, Mr. Chase. I've been waiting for this opportunity for us to talk."

"Who is that?" Chase responded in a trembling voice. "Keith?"

"No, Mr. Rogers and Miss O'Malley are quite safe. This is justice, Mr. Chase. I know who you are ... and what you are. And I've come for vengeance."

"I don't know what you're talking about ... you ... you've made a mistake."

"No, you're the one who made a mistake ... when you started killing!"

"What? I've never killed anyone!"

The Jackal raised his voice even louder, knowing it would be echoing in the sound-proof booth.

"For one, you killed me, Chase! The time for lies is over!"

"No ... no ..."

"Look behind the booth ... because I am here!"

The Jackal reached and flicked on a spotlight to shine on the normally dark space behind the recording booth. Chase spun around and screamed in fear when he saw the ghostly white face of Chief Morgan.

When the lights had gone out, Jennifer Jones had almost emerged from her hiding space in the equipment room. She had snuck into the small room after climbing the stairs. Stuck among various sound effects devices, microphones and other equipment, she had been able to watch the proceedings by leaving the door slightly open.

As she was about to open the door, she had heard the deep voice reassure Keith and Margaret. *The Red Jackal,* was her first thought. Her second was to curse herself for not bringing a camera with her from the newsroom. *A chance to finally get proof and I'm here with nothing to see, sitting in the dark.*

She heard the presumed Jackal direct the two to the elevator and then listened with growing interest to the exchange between Harrison Chase and the man at the control panel. *Is Chase the killer?* She would have never considered it. She didn't know the young man well, but he just seemed too quiet to be any trouble.

She slipped quietly out of the closet and eased closer to the booth, moving slowly and carefully as she tried to remember the layout of the room. She started to pull out her notebook, then decided it would do her no good in the darkness, even as her eyes were starting to adjust. Luckily, the *Gazette's* star reporter had a great memory, honed by several years of covering major news stories in the Twin Cities.

"For one, you killed me, Chase! The time for lies is over!"

"No ... no ..."

"Look behind the booth ... because I am here!"

Jennifer looked toward the booth herself, then let out a scream that echoed that of Chase.

In the soundproof booth, Chase didn't hear Jennifer's scream, but the Jackal did. Like his hearing, his vision had been improved thanks to his time in Egypt. He clearly saw her even as he extinguished the light and the studio plunged back into darkness.

Jennifer! Damn that woman!

This had not been expected. He took his hand off the microphone so Chase wouldn't hear him.

"I see you Miss Jones. I don't have time to deal with you right now ... just stay out of this."

He could hear Chase repeatedly muttering, "No ... no," in the booth.

He triggered the microphone again. "Yes, Mr. Chase. You killed me and your time of reckoning has come. Justice has come for you!"

As he finished, the Jackal turned on all the lights in the booth, flooding it with brightness.

"I'm hear to escort you to the next life to face justice. The innocent men you have killed demand it!"

"No!" Chase shouted as he lunged for the door of the recording booth, only to find it wouldn't open as he struggled with the knob.

"YES!" the Jackal increased his volume again, with the help of the station's equipment. "Admit your crimes now or face the wrath of the spirit world!"

"I see you Miss Jones. I don't have time to deal with you right now ... just stay out of this."

Jennifer ignored the instructions of the Jackal – she was sure it was him now – and continued moving toward the booth. Looking through the two glass walls of the booth from the far side, she had seen someone back there. She was going to find out who it was. *Who is helping the Red Jackal?*

Her eyes had pretty much adjusted to the darkness and she could dimly make out the corner of the booth. She was about to reach out, planning to feel her way around to the back when the bright lights of the suddenly lit booth momentarily blinded her. She stumbled backwards, tripped over a rat's nest of cords and fell to the floor, hitting her head with a resounding *thunk*.

The Red Jackal heard Jennifer trip and fell and turned just in time to see her land awkwardly. When she didn't rise from the floor he released the microphone and started in her direction, only to be stopped by the voice of Chief Morgan.

"I've got her. Finish it!"

The Jackal nodded once, turned back toward Chase and triggered the intercom.

"I'm done waiting, Harrison Chase!"

The Jackal reached into his pocket, and pressed the button on a small remote control. A wall of flames erupted outside the booth. Or what – thanks to Geoffrey – *appeared* to be a wall of flames.

"Your time is up – I take you for judgement in Hell!"

Chase fell to his knees and began sobbing.

"No, no ... it's all true. I killed all of you. Chief Morgan, Franklin, Deppler, James, the fool in Duluth. I did all of it ... just don't take me away, no ..."

Chase wrapped his arms around himself, curling up in a sobbing ball. The Jackal released the microphone, pressed the stop button on the recording and turned off the flame projection.

He pivoted toward where Morgan kneeled next to Jennifer, who was moaning slightly.

"She took a nasty knock on the head, but I think she's going to have nothing worse than a headache," Morgan said.

"Good," the Jackal said gruffly. "You should have everything you need, Chief. Everything he said was recorded … and nothing else. As far as anyone who listens will know, he just went a little nuts when the lights went out. I trust you'll be able to get what you need."

Chief Morgan smiled grimly. "This may not hold up in court, but I'm not sure we'll make it that far, anyway. He may be headed to an asylum." He glanced down as Jennifer moaned again and stirred slightly. "You better go."

"Until we meet again, Chief Morgan," the Jackal said, offering a quick two-fingered salute before racing away.

First she heard a multitude of voices and movement, then a single voice made its way through the fog.

"Miss Jones … Miss Jones …"

Jennifer opened her eyes, then quickly closed them again as she looked up into the light in front of her face. She opened them more slowly this time to see Dr. Springfield with a small penlight.

"Ahh, good. There we are. I understand you took quite a spill. I was waiting downstairs with the police when Chief Morgan called us to come up."

Jennifer shook her head in an attempt to clear the cobwebs and was immediately hit by a wave of dizziness.

"Whoa, Miss Jones. Not a good idea. You hit your head but good. Let's sit up here," he said as he pulled a chair over toward the reporter.

She eased herself up slowly and sat in the chair. She now saw that the studio was filled with officers from the city, county and state. "Chief Morgan? I thought he was in the hospital."

Springfield smiled. "Ahh, that was a bit of deception. You see, he … well, that's really not my place to say, especially to a reporter.

"I think you're going to be fine, young lady, but let's be careful about stumbling around in the dark from now on."

Jennifer choked back her retort at his young lady comment when she saw Chief Morgan coming over.

"Where's the Red Jackal?" she asked as soon as he reached her.

The chief looked at her with confusion on his face and shook his head. "The Red Jackal? You mean that vigilante?"

"He was here. I heard him *and* saw him. He's the one who got Chase to confess."

"Really?" the chief responded. "I wouldn't know about that. By the time I got here, you were unconscious on the floor and Chase was sobbing in the booth. Something about seeing my ghost or the devil or something. Apparently when the power went out, the door to the booth got jammed and he just snapped. The whole thing was recorded … he confessed to everything, but there are no other voices on the tape. Speaking of which, I need to get back to the station so we can question him some more. Doctor, why don't you take Miss Jones to the hospital and make sure she gets fully checked out."

"Wait!" Jennifer yelled as Morgan started away.

He turned back in her direction. "Yes, Miss Jones?"

"What about Keith Rogers and Margaret O'Malley. Surely they saw something."

"No, I don't think so. They said when the power went out and they realized Chase was stuck in the booth they went to get help. When they got to the lobby, I heard the radio call and came right up here. I just managed to get here a minute before the rest of the officers. They didn't say anything about this Red Jackal of yours."

It had taken several hours for the police to finish their work at the *Gazette* building, but the newsroom was back to normal by Saturday morning. Jennifer Jones had already started on her story about the arrest, with plans to head back to the courthouse where Chief Morgan and other officials were expected to have a press conference soon.

Over her objections, there would be no mention of the Red Jackal. Both Blake and city editor Rod Stanley had agreed there wasn't enough proof that the Jackal had been there.

Lincoln had come to visit Blake to let him know that he had received word that Keith Rogers was completely exonerated. Harrison Chase had signed a confession Friday night without any objection. His spirit had been broken in the recording booth. Now that he was no longer opposing counsel, Lincoln had received an off-the-record update from one of the assistant state's attorneys.

"It's a bizarre story," he said. "He insists that the ghost of Chief Morgan made him confess – despite the fact that Morgan is alive and well.

"Anyway, it started out as a pretty simple idea. Somehow he got it in his head that the only thing standing between him and radio stardom was Kent Franklin. So he decided to kill him. The other killings were just meant to be a smokescreen, to make it look like the work of some crazy spree killer. Then, it seems … I guess you would say, it just got away from him."

They both looked up at the sound of a knock on the closed door. Through the glass wall, Blake could see that it was David, back from his fishing trip on Lake Ludlow. He gestured for him to come in.

David and Lincoln exchanged greetings as David sat down, joining Lincoln in the seats opposite Blake's desk.

"I read the *Duluth Herald* on the train ride down – what else is going on that wasn't in there?"

Blake and the attorney quickly filled David in on all the recent developments, including Rogers's exoneration and Chase's confession.

"All right, gentlemen," Lincoln said, standing up after they finished the update. "Today is supposed to be my day off. Myra's got a list of chores I need to get done. Nothing personal, but I'm hoping this is the end of our daily meetings for a while, Blake."

Blake and David said their goodbyes and watched the attorney leave the office and start walking through the newsroom.

"Now, what else does the Red Jackal have to add?" David asked as he turned back toward his brother.

"I really couldn't tell you. Apparently there's some crazy rumor that the Red Jackal was involved, but you know how those things go ..."

"Uh huh." David leaned forward. "Let me ask you this ... how did you know it was Chase?"

"The truth is that most crimes aren't senseless. They have some motivation, whether it be love, greed, need, whatever it may be. When the Franklin murder was the only one we knew about, I asked myself who benefited? Then, as the other crimes were revealed, I put that aside. But something kept drawing me back. Then I remembered something Rogers had said earlier – that Chase had gone home for the 4th of July week. And anyone from Hermantown is going to know Duluth.

"The truth is I wasn't completely sure until he rigged the microphone. The goal was to trap him with that and he couldn't pass up the opportunity."

"And that's another thing," David said. "How did you know that was going to work?"

"There were only three episodes that hadn't been used as an inspiration for the killings. I took the odds that he wasn't going to try to feed Morgan to a cage full of lions or kill him with the magic sword box. Once we were ready for the microphone to malfunction, it was no problem to outfit the chief with gloves and shoes from Geoffrey that would ground the charge."

"I tell you, I go away for a week and I miss all the excitement."

"Fine, next year, you stay down here for the 4th. I'll go fishing and you can take care of the homicidal maniacs."

"Ahh, but the mask would never fit me, big brother. Your head is much too big."

A Tip of the Cowl

This story brings to life the idea that first launched the creation of the Red Jackal.

It was the discovery of abandoned tunnels under the city of Chaska, Minn., that inspired the character. Those tunnels – although almost certainly used as part of the brick industry – prompted my mind running in the direction of pulp heroes and secret lairs.

Eventually, that character became the Red Jackal, while Chaska became the fictional and much larger city of Brickton, although retaining some of its characteristics and history.

Shadow Street

Nobody cared when denizens of skid row started disappearing ... until the Red Jackal took the case!

I

"*HELP!*"

The Red Jackal heard the scream of the woman – just a block to the east, he judged. He rose from his crouch overlooking the Gateway District flophouse and headed in that direction, crossing rooftop to rooftop.

"Help! Help! I'm being mugged!"

He was headed in the right direction. The Jackal sped up. The overcast night, with not a functioning streetlight to be found here on Minneapolis's skid row, made it difficult to see. As he reached the alley between two run-down illegal saloons, he was able to make out what appeared to be a young woman struggling with three men.

The Jackal leapt from the roof on the north side of the alley, landing behind the largest of the three men, who dwarfed the Jackal's 6-foot frame. The Jackal quickly delivered a powerful uppercut to his jaw, leaving him a moaning heap on the trash-strewn pavement. He glanced briefly at the woman, grabbing her with one hand and sending her clear of the fight. *Something familiar about her*, ran quickly through his mind.

He spun to face the second man, delivering a kick to the man's soft stomach and sending him crashing into the wall of the alley. He turned to the final man, who was holding up his hands and backing away, "No, no, mister ..." he whimpered. It was not an unusual reaction. The scarlet mask and jackal insignia struck fear into most of the criminal element in the Twin Cities.

"Stop! Enough!" the woman's voice rang out as the Jackal took a step toward the last attacker. He looked behind him to see her crouching over the man crumpled against the wall. The man was conscious, but obviously dazed. The Jackal heard a clatter behind him and looked to see the uninjured mugger drop something and run down the alley.

"You really hurt them," the woman said with an accusing tone in her voice, her back still to him as she tended to the injured man.

Confusion and anger battled in his voice. "Well, yes, I tend to do that when I see someone being attacked, Miss."

"I didn't expect you to be that fast," she replied defensively. As she stood up and turned around, the light leaking from the illegal speakeasy at the head of the alley illuminated her features. The Jackal saw she was young, with a classically beautiful face and short blond hair – in fact, she was generally regarded as one of the most eligible women in the Twin Cities.

"Hello, Miss Sullivan," he said. "I have a feeling there's more than a mugging going on here?"

Elaine Sullivan was the only child of Ellis Sullivan, the founder of Sullivan's Department Store and one of the wealthiest men in Minnesota. The Red Jackal had met the younger Sullivan earlier that year when she was kidnapped by the Cooper Gang, a notorious band of bank robbers. The Red Jackal had rescued the heiress and foiled the gang's attempt at a big payday from her millionaire father.

"That attack was staged for your benefit," Elaine responded. "These men aren't guilty of anything other than trying to help me get your attention."

Both men were now standing under their own power, albeit unsteadily. Their rheumy eyes and worn clothing indicated they were two of the many poor living on skid row.

"This is Ernie," Elaine indicated the larger of the two, a black man with gray facial hair, who looked to be in his 50s. "This is Kurt," gesturing at the second man, a white man who could have been anywhere from 30 to 70 years old. "Thank you, both of you. I'm sorry you got hurt. That wasn't my intent."

"We know that, Miss Sullivan," Ernie – the one he had knocked down when he jumped from the roof – responded. Turning to the Jackal, he said, "You pack one hell of a punch, mister. I used to be a fighter and it takes a lot to knock me down."

"I'm sorry both of you were hurt as well, but does someone want to tell me what's going here?"

Elaine nodded. "Along with Gerald – the man you scared off – they've been helping me try to find you. We've been staging these attacks for three nights. It was honestly the only way I could think of to get your attention. It's not like I can call the operator and ask to be connected to The Red Jackal.

"We may have underestimated how quickly you would jump into the fray," she added sheepishly.

"That's a dangerous game, Miss Sullivan, especially in this neighborhood," he responded sharply. "You and your friends could have been seriously hurt."

He took a breath, and added, in a calmer tone, "I'm assuming this has to do with more than my charming personality? Why are you trying to track me down?"

"There's someone killing us, that's why!" the previous silent Kurt answered, quickly sobering the Jackal.

He looked questioningly at Elaine.

"He's right," she said. "Well, at least I think he is. Residents of the district are disappearing. The authorities don't care and people are vanishing. We need your help."

The Jackal looked around the alley, which offered little in the way of privacy or comfort. He reached into his pocket, removing a small black box, and pushed a button. "This sounds like a longer discussion. May I suggest we talk elsewhere?"

Elaine tilted her head slightly in thought. "I suppose we could find somewhere. There might be a room in the mission we could use, or ..." She trailed off at the sound of a vehicle approaching the alley.

A large, entirely black Packard appeared at the entrance of the alley, running with no lights. The Jackal pointed at the car. "I had an alternative in mind."

II

ELAINE SULLIVAN and the Red Jackal were in the rear compartment of his heavily modified Packard sedan. Elaine had instructed Ernie and Kurt to return to the nearby St. Vincent Mission, warning them to be cautious. The two men had been reluctant to leave her, but she had assured them she would be safe with the vigilante.

Unseen in the front seat was Geoffrey, Blake Randolph's long-time trusted driver and valet. He was silently piloting the car through the streets of Minneapolis. The blackout windows and soundproofing of the fortress on wheels guaranteed their privacy as they discussed the strange disappearances.

Although a member of St. Paul's high society, Elaine Sullivan was well-known for her volunteer work in the worst areas of the Twin Cities. She worked several days a week at the St. Vincent Mission in the Gateway District. She was trusted by the residents of the area, most of whom had fallen out of notice of any of the city's more prominent citizens.

The disappearances had been happening for several weeks, but Elaine had only become aware of the problem in the last few days. Ernie brought it to her attention after a friend of his had vanished.

"At first, nobody really noticed," she said. "After all, the population of the Gateway District is by its nature a transient one. People come, people go."

"But this is different?"

"Yes, some of these men are long-time residents of the district," she said. "They've lived here for years, some of them in the same rooming houses for a decade or more. Then, suddenly, they're just gone. To outsiders, they may seem like faceless bums, but there is a community here."

She had talked to volunteers at several of the various religious and community organizations working in the Gateway District and found similar stories. Men, most over 40, were simply disappearing. It appeared that no women had been taken. Rumors were flying among the residents of the district. Some claimed to have seen a strange green truck driving around at odd times of the night. Others told tales of a well-dressed man being spotted talking to some of the men who later disappeared. Still others blamed the government, claiming the men were being taken for some sort of strange experiment. For every man who disappeared there were a dozen strange rumors.

"As best I can tell, more than a dozen men have disappeared in the last month or so, but it's hard to know for sure, of course. It could be even more. Nobody really keeps track of everyone down here. By the time someone ends up in the district, it's easy for them to disappear and not be noticed."

The Jackal knew that Elaine was right, that for many the poor became invisible, the denizens of skid row an urban scourge to be ignored.

"And the police?" he asked, anticipating the answer.

The police departments in both Minneapolis and St. Paul had been riddled with corruption for decades thanks to an agreement with organized crime figures. Recent additions to the departments were working hard to change that, but continued to be resisted by the entrenched culture of corruption.

"The police are chronically understaffed here, so the easiest explanation is what they choose to accept: that these men just moved on to another city or neighborhood, or that they'll turn up someday after a drinking binge. You know how our civic leaders feel about this neighborhood – they'd be content to see the entire area bulldozed and pushed into the Mississippi."

"I think you overstate the case, but I understand your point. Let me see what I can find out." He removed a small card from his scarlet suit. "You can call this number the next time you need to reach me. My assistant will always know where to find me. It will be much more effective than hoping I stumble upon a fictitious assault.

"Where would you like us to drop you, Miss Sullivan?"

"Back at the mission. My driver is waiting for me there."

The Jackal pressed a button below the black divider that separated the front and rear compartments of the Packard.

"The mission," he said.

As the Packard continued toward the mission, he turned to look at Elaine, "I have to admit I'm surprised your father has allowed you to continue your work after your ordeal this spring."

"My father *allows* me to do nothing. I don't need his permission – but he agrees with me that my work here is important. It's why he has funded so much of the operation of the mission. I have agreed to be more careful in my work and no longer take streetcars to and from the mission."

The Packard slowed to a stop and a red light above the intercom button flashed.

"It appears we have arrived back at the mission, Miss Sullivan," the Jackal said, He stepped out of the car, determined with a glance that the street and sidewalk were empty, and offered his hand to Elaine to help her out of the vehicle.

"I'll be in touch," he told her, waiting until she reached the door to the mission before climbing back into the Packard. Once inside, he again pressed the intercom button.

"Take us home Geoffrey. I've got a breakfast appointment with Lt. McDaniels."

"This is unacceptable! You said a week ago you had a breakthrough! Now this?"

The doctor jumped at the voice behind him and spun around to see his employer wheeling toward him out of the dark passageway, followed by a thin, ferret-faced, impeccably dressed man. Maxwell was his employer's nephew – his only living relative – and a conniving, cowardly, twit. *You can spend as much money on clothes as you want and grow yourself a mustache, but you're still one ugly bastard*, the doctor thought.

The doctor pushed his glasses back on his nose as he responded: "Yes, yes, I thought we had it taken care of, you see, we had—"

From the smug smile on Maxwell's face, it was clear how he had heard the news of the latest setback. The doctor was convinced he was rooting for failure in order to more quickly receive his inheritance.

"Well, obviously you thought wrong!" The deep, strong voice

seemed contradictory to the withered body from whence it came.

He's getting worse. His body is failing him, the doctor thought to himself. He was quite content to let the man die, but if his employer knew that, his service would not end well for the doctor.

"I don't want excuses! Take care of it!" His voice rose as he yelled that last, then a coughing fit racked his withered body, shaking the wheelchair. As he gasped for air, Maxwell took a step toward him, but stopped when his uncle waved his hand at him. He grabbed a mask from a cubby on the side of the chair, inhaled deeply from the oxygen canister and calmed his breathing.

"Enough," he rasped. "I'm running out of time and so are you!"

The electronic chair pivoted silently and glided out of the room, with Maxwell trailing behind him. The doctor turned back to his table. The man in front of him moaned, but the straps holding him snugly to the table ensured he would not be able to move.

The doctor picked up the syringe he had dropped when his employer startled him. He was glad to see it hadn't been damaged.

"Now, my friend," he muttered under his breath. "Let's see if you have any more luck than your brethren."

He plunged the needle into the man's heart and stepped back to see what happened.

III

AT 7 A.M. the next morning, a tall, fit, black-haired man walked into the Eastside Diner. The greasy spoon was located, oddly enough, on the far west side of Minneapolis. The coffee was an effective alternative to paint thinner, the food was heartburn-inducing and the grill probably hadn't been cleaned since the current president's cousin was living in the White House.

To the non-descript visitor, it offered exactly one inducement: Lt. Brian McDaniels of the Minneapolis Police Department ate breakfast there every morning. Spotting McDaniels, Blake Randolph – unrecognizable in one of his many disguises – made his way to the corner booth and slid in across from the officer.

"If it isn't my favorite vigilante," McDaniels said as he looked up from his paper. "And what brings you to ruin the morning of this humble civil servant today?"

McDaniels was a veteran of the department, a second-generation police officer and an honest one to boot. He had met the Red Jackal years earlier when he was walking a beat along Hennepin Ave. It was several years before he knew his real identity, discovered only when he saved a grievously wounded Jackal from certain death. He was one of the trusted few who knew Blake Randolph's secret. Now he was a top detective on the force and a trusted source. Long frustrated with the corruption he faced in the department, he recognized that the Jackal could take care of problems he could not.

"Good morning, Lieutenant. And how is the coffee this morning?"

"As bad as always."

"And the eggs?"

"Horrendous."

"And you eat here why?"

"Because usually it means nobody bothers me while I eat breakfast. Now, do you want to continue talking about my morning habits or did you have something else in mind? Perhaps the Series?" he said, holding up the sports section of the *Minneapolis Tribune*. "The Giants should handle the Senators pretty easily, if you ask me. That Carl Hubbell is pretty damn good."

"Actually I wanted to talk about the disappearances in the Gateway District."

That prompted McDaniels to set the paper down and looked

directly at Blake. His furrowed eyebrows showed his confusion.

"What the hell are you talking about?"

Blake proceeded to fill the lieutenant in on all the information he had been provided by Elaine Sullivan, leaving her name out of it for now. As he continued, McDaniels tapping his hands on the table, loudly enough to draw a glance from the waitress at the counter, who quickly looked away again.

"There's something ... something ... familiar about that ..." McDaniels said, almost to himself.

Blake looked at him curiously. "You mean—" McDaniels waved him to silence with an annoyed look on his face. He shut up and sat silently for almost 60 seconds, watching McDaniels work on the problem.

"Chicago," he said finally. "Chicago," he said again, waving his finger and looking down at the table.

"Care to enlighten me, Lieutenant?"

"A few years ago I met a Chicago police detective – a fellow mick by the name of O'Toole – who was trying to track down one of Capone's associates who was rumored to be hiding up here. He didn't make any progress through official channels, of course, but a desk sergeant directed him my way. Turned out to be nothing – the guy wasn't up here – but we ended up talking over dinner.

"He told me about this strange case where hobos had been disappearing from the south side of Chicago. The best he could figure it might have been as many as 30 of them over five or six months, then it just stopped. He had looked into it, but, frankly, nobody really cared and he was told to leave it alone, especially since the problem seemed to have ended.

"This had to be 1925, 1926 when it was happening. Years later it still bothered him. He kept following up on his own time, but never really got anywhere.

"It was that 'well-dressed' man comment that reminded me. Several people said there was a man, definitely too wealthy to be spending time there, who was around a lot for those few months. He was apparently handing out money, hiring people for odd jobs or something like that."

"That can't be a coincidence. How do we get ahold of this detective?"

"We don't," McDaniels replied. "He's dead. He got gunned down by some of Capone's crew a few months after I met him. That's what he got for being an honest cop."

From the grave look on his face, Blake knew he was remembering what had happened to his own father. The senior McDaniels had been a beat cop in St. Paul who dared to challenge the corrupt O'Connor system that allowed criminals safe haven in the capital city. His reward had been to be found in an alley with two bullets in his back. The case was closed in less than a week as an unsolved murder, blamed on criminals unknown. The then 14-year-old McDaniels son hadn't forgotten the lesson of that murder. It was why he was careful to keep his cooperation with the Red Jackal quiet.

McDaniels slapped the table again, as if trying to clear the memory. "I'll see what I can find out, but don't get your hopes up," he said. "The odds of getting any official attention on this are pretty slim. I assume the Red Jackal will be doing his usual lurking in shadows and general intimidation of the criminal element?"

Blake chucked. "That would be the plan," he said. "You know how to contact me. Anything you can find out, Lieutenant, might be helpful."

He slid out of the booth and made his way out of the eatery and out onto the street, a perfectly forgettable man, barely noticed by the other diners.

IV

AFTER DEPARTING the Eastside Diner, Blake Randolph again changed his appearance, using one of the many hideaways he kept for just such purposes. He opted this time for a rundown look that would make him look at home at the St. Vincent Mission.

After Geoffrey dropped him off at the edge of the district, the incognito Jackal made his way to the mission. He knew Elaine Sullivan would not be there today, and he hoped to have a chance to gather more information about the residents of the neighborhood.

When he opened the door, the Jackal spotted Ernie mopping the floor in the dining hall. Besides a group of five men sitting at a table on one side of the room, the mission's front room was empty.

Ernie looked up as he entered. "Sorry, friend, you missed breakfast. If you come back at 12 there will be lunch. There's still hot coffee if you want it," he said, nodding to a pot at the side of the hall.

"Actually, I was hoping to talk to you, friend," he said in a low voice as he drew close to Ernie. "I'm Miss Sullivan's friend from last night."

Ernie's eyes went wide. "You mean you're the Red—"

The Jackal held up his hand. "Let's just call me Jack for now."

"Yeah, sure, whatever you say. How can I help? Did you learn something?"

"A little bit, maybe. I just want to get some more information and I think you can help me."

Ernie looked around the room, taking in the mostly empty space. "Sure, I guess that I can do that. Just let me finish mopping in here. Uh, why don't you grab some coffee and we can talk over there," he said pointing to an empty table in the back of the room, as far away from the other men as possible.

"Jack" poured himself a cup of coffee and headed to the table Ernie had indicated. He realized as he did so that two of the men on the other side of the room were Gerald and Kurt, the other counterfeit muggers from the previous evening. He didn't recognize the other men.

Ernie had been with his friend shortly before he disappeared and he was hoping the man could remember more details about that day. After a few minutes, Ernie wheeled the mop and bucket to the kitchen, then returned and joined him at the table.

"I told Sister Katherine you were a friend of mine from Duluth," he said. "I lived up there for a while before I came down here. She won't mind if we take some time to talk."

The Jackal took a sip of the coffee and grimaced. It was better than the Eastside Diner, but that was about the only good thing that could be said about it.

Ernie stifled a laugh. "I guess I should have warned you about that. Most of us are just happy to have something warm to drink."

The Jackal joined him in chuckling. "I've had worse, but yeah, it's pretty bad. So, Ernie, you know I never even got your last name."

"Truth is, uh, Jack, that there's not much call for last names around here. But it's Bailey."

"Wait a minute. Ernie Bailey? You 'used to be a fighter'? You're that Ernie Bailey?"

"Uh, yes, sir, that's me," Ernie replied, looking down in embarrassment.

The Jackal realized with a start just how much abuse Ernie had taken. The man he had taken to be in his 50s was still a few years short of 40.

"But how did you end up here? You were almost the champ. I saw you fight Gene Souza when I was in St. Louis after the war. You gave him a great fight. Should have won, in my opinion."

Ernie shrugged his shoulders. "Pretty typical story, I guess.

Black boxers don't get a lot of chances. I lost that fight, then another, then another. After that, things just … kind of fell apart. I kept fighting, but the purses got smaller and smaller, and well, I started drinking, and then … that was that.

"Not a lot of jobs for drunk, black, ex-boxers. Eventually I wound up working at the harbor in Duluth, then I lost that job, too, and found my way to Minneapolis. Just about drank myself to death before I met Sister Katherine and Miss Sullivan."

He brightened at that. "Haven't had a drink in more than a year, now, though. That's part of my deal with Sister Katherine. I can work here as long as I stay sober."

"So I took down a guy who almost took out the future heavyweight champ. Guess I should be proud of that."

Ernie let loose a full, deep laugh. "Only because Miss Sullivan told us not to fight back."

The Jackal smiled at that, then turned serious.

"I hope you can help me with some more information, Ernie. Tell me about your friend who was taken."

The man, known simply as Cap, was a long-time resident of the district, moving from rooming house to rooming house. Sometimes he slept on the street when he couldn't come up with even the rent for one of the flophouses. Shortly after Ernie arrived in Minneapolis, he had rescued Cap from a beating. Cap had thanked him by introducing Ernie to the St. Vincent Mission.

"I owe him my life," he finished. "If I hadn't … well, I'd probably have been dead in a gutter somewhere."

"When was the last time you saw him?"

"It was about a week ago," Ernie said. "Cap told me he had a big deal lined up. Some great job that was going to make him enough money to pay his way for the rest of the year. He said it had something to do with this guy he was talking to the day before, but I couldn't tell anyone because he didn't want anyone else horning in on his action. He wouldn't tell me much.

"Do you know who this man was?"

"No, the afternoon before I came out of the mission and saw him talking to a man down the block, but I couldn't really see anything, and then he took off."

"You might be surprised by how much you saw. Let's try to remember ..."

"I'll do my best, Jack, but sometimes it's hard for me to remember things these days. The booze and the shots to the head ..." he shook his head as if trying to clear it of cobwebs.

"I can help with that, Ernie, if you trust me. Just clear your head and listen to my voice ..."

The Jackal continued to speak in a soft tone, helping Ernie slip into a trance. It was one of the many abilities he had found himself to have since his time in Egypt. In the particularly weak-minded, he was even able to control their thoughts, driving them to action or erasing all memory of their interaction with the Jackal. He had no desire to do that to Ernie, but even if he had The Jackal sensed a strong will behind the man's gentle exterior. Despite the beating his body had taken – both in and out of the ring – there was a core of mental steel to this man.

The memory holds secrets beyond what most people realize, the Jackal knew. And Ernie was no exception. Precise questions and probing revealed a wealth of information. That man had been well-dressed, in a dark overcoat, white shirt, red scarf around his neck. He had stood about the same height as Cap – based on Ernie's estimation, that put him at roughly 5'10" or 5'9". Average build, maybe a little on the thin side. Dark brown or black hair; Homburg hat. Clean-shaven, with the exception of a pencil-thin mustache. The man had quickly slipped into his black sedan when he saw Ernie approaching.

"We're done, Ernie," the Jackal said.

"Huh?" the former boxer said as he blinked his eyes and came back to the present. "That was strange. But it worked?"

"I think so," the Jackal said, holding his hand out to Ernie as he rose from the table.

A surprised Ernie looked at his hand for a second before shaking it. "Good. There's something scary going on out there. I don't know what it is and I don't know if anyone cares, but something is happening."

"We're going to figure it out, Ernie. You think of anything else or hear anything else, tell Miss Sullivan. She knows how to get ahold of me. And watch yourself. You saw this man and that may be enough to cause you trouble."

V

BY 2 P.M. that afternoon, Blake Randolph, appearing as himself for the first time that day, was at his desk at the *Brickton Gazette*, the paper his family owned and ran. Blake had been the publisher of the paper since his father's death and helped grow the *Gazette* to the fourth-largest paper in Minnesota.

There was a knock on his door, and Blake looked up to see his younger brother, David, at the door. David Randolph, 12 years younger than Blake, was taking over many of the day-to-day operations of the family's businesses.

"Kate said you wanted to see me?"

"Yes, come on in," Blake said, beckoning with his hand. "You still keep in touch with Sandy Freeman? Is he still at the *Tribune*?"

Freeman had been a fraternity brother of David's at the University of Chicago who had embarked on a journalism career in the city after graduation.

"It's been a couple of months, but, yeah, as far as I know, he's still working there. Last I heard he was still writing obituaries. Why?"

"Those disappearances in the Gateway District might be related to an earlier case in Chicago. Lt. McDaniels said it rang a bell, but the detective who told him about it was killed by Capone's gang. I'm hoping somebody at the *Tribune* might remember something about it."

"Well, let's see, why don't we?"

After navigating long distance and the operator at the *Tribune*, David finally ascertained that Freeman still worked at the paper. It took almost 10 minutes, but they finally tracked down the writer – who was still reporting the deaths of those great and small. David explained the situation to him.

"Before my time, obviously, but the one you need to talk to is Milo. He runs the morgue here. If we wrote about it, he's going to know."

As newspapermen themselves, both David and Blake knew that in this case "morgue" meant a repository for old articles, not dead bodies.

It took another five minutes, but Milo was finally available on the other end of the crackling long-distance lines. Blake took over and shared the details he knew, including the death of the detective.

"I remember that O'Toole fellow, that's for sure. In fact, that's the reason I remember those cases you're talking about. We didn't write much about it. Bums disappearing on the south side don't sell papers.

"But that O'Toole – he kept after it. Annoyed the hacks in the newsroom and was always coming down here asking me for old stories."

As it turned out, there had been little to find in the paper, except for two instances where out-of-town family had come to the city looking for answers about their missing relative. Those families hadn't seemed to get anywhere, either, Milo said. Just as with the disappearances in Minneapolis, these cases had escaped notice by most people. However, Milo clearly didn't get a lot of visitors in the morgue and was willing to continue talking about O'Toole.

Blake was trying to extricate himself from the conversation, when one comment caught his attention.

"It's a shame what happened to him. He was like a dog with

a bone, but a nice fellow. I always wondered if maybe he had been on to something after all. Otherwise, why kill him?"

That caught the attention of Blake, who thought maybe he had misheard him over the hisses and cracks of the long-distance line.

"Wait, say that again," Blake said. "I thought Capone had O'Toole killed?"

"Sure, that was the story, but it doesn't make a lot of sense. This was late 1930; Capone was already in trouble with his taxes, the Philadelphia weapons charge, the Miami case. It just doesn't read true that Capone would bother at that point. And honestly, in Chicago, one honest cop was never going to be more than a minor annoyance to Capone. But it made a nice way to wrap it up and get the case off the books."

With that new piece of information, Blake thanked him for his time and hung up.

"You think he's right?" David asked. "Or does he just have an overactive imagination?"

"Hard to say, but worth thinking about. Lt. McDaniels might be able to dig up some more information."

A quick call to police headquarters determined that McDaniels wasn't at the station. Blake said he would try to track him down later that night.

"Not so fast, big brother. You've got plans tonight – the Civic Foundation Feed the Hungry Dinner?"

"Oh, God. That's tonight …"

The Civic Foundation was a group of business and local leaders in the Twin Cities that was working to combat poverty, hunger and other fallout of the Depression. The Randolph family was one of its largest benefactors. As much as Blake hated events like this, he knew it was a good cause, worthy of the family's support. If he didn't attend, he would be conspicuous by his absence.

"Yes, and you've got less than two hours to get dressed and

get back here. Geoffrey has your tuxedo ready at the house and the car is waiting for you downstairs."

"I'd like to point out once again that we all could write very generous checks to the foundation, cancel the dinner and everybody wins."

"Alas, dear brother, some of the wealthy of our community are not as virtuous as you and must be plied with food and drink to loosen their purses."

Blake threw up his hands in surrender. "Fine. Monkey suit, here I come."

The doctor and Maxwell were waiting in the abandoned bakery when their visitor stepped through the door.

"Why didn't you do what we told you to?" Maxwell asked, waving a .38 special as he spoke.

"I … I …" the man stammered. "I told you I didn't want to kill Miss Sullivan."

The doctor started to move closer, then grimaced and stepped back again as the pungent mix of cheap booze and body odor overwhelmed him. *Disgusting creature*, he thought to himself.

"As it turns out, your cowardice has probably paid off. Killing her would have brought us attention we didn't need. *I* never thought it was a good idea," he said, glancing meaningfully at Maxwell.

"She was gonna blab to that Red Jackal guy," Maxwell whined. "Now we got to worry about him!"

"Shut up, Maxwell. And stop waving that thing around. You're going to shoot somebody."

Maxwell glared at him, but sat down on a discarded crate to pout.

The doctor turned back to their visitor.

"We're almost done here. I just need two or three more subject for my … tests. What do you have for me?"

"Yeah, I can find guys, no problem, Doc, but …"

"But what?"

"Cap, one of the guys you took last week, well …"

Maxwell leaped off the crate and pushed his pistol in the man's face. "Well what, you stinking bum?"

The words came rushing out. "Ernie, one of his friends, saw you guys take him and he told the Red Jackal about it and now the Red Jackal's going to catch us and kill all of us — "

"SHUT UP!" Maxwell lifted his hand, but the doctor grabbed his arm before he could finish his strike.

"Enough! Both of you!" He removed his hat and ran his hand over his bald head.

"Fine. I'm not worried about some Robin Hood wannabee running around in his pajamas. But just to be on the safe side … let's take care of this … Ernie, was it?" At the bum's quick nod, he continued. "I'm going to keep this simple for you. Tonight you will …"

VI

THANKS TO the efficiency of Geoffrey, Blake made it back to the *Gazette* offices with 10 minutes to spare, where he found David waiting for him in the ground floor lobby.

"And why exactly are we coming back here instead of going directly to the Plaza?" Blake asked his brother.

David just pointed across the lobby. Emerging from the elevator was Jennifer Jones, star reporter for the *Gazette*, stunning in a floor-length, form-fitting dress. It was a radically different look for the usually all-business appearance of the dedicated journalist.

"What? I—"

David smiled. "Did I forget to mention you had a date

tonight? The whole back and forth was getting to be a bit much so I just took some initiative. … And you may want to stop staring."

"There are a million reasons why this won't work," Blake whispered back. "No. 1 would happen to be that she is dedicated to unmasking the Red Jackal!"

Jennifer's all-too-familiar, teasing smile was on her face as she drew near. "Well, good evening, Chief," she said as she held out her arm. "Shall we?"

The trio headed out to the street where Geoffrey waited with the car.

As the evening continues, despite his misgivings, Blake was surprised to find himself enjoying the night. The speeches were short, he had to make little of the small talk he so abhorred and Jennifer was an enchanting dinner companion. When he allowed himself to admit it, he knew he had feelings for the woman he had known since childhood. Once the annoying younger sister of his best friend and fellow soldier, she was now not only his best reporter, but one of the most important people in his life. But he also knew that his identity as the Red Jackal meant anyone that was close to him would be in danger if they knew his secret. But maybe …

"Blake, I figured we would see you here."

The familiar booming voice of U.S. Senator Victor Charles roused him from his thoughts.

"Senator Charles, a pleasure," he said, holding out his hand. "And I'm sure you remember Jennifer Jones, one of our best reporters."

"Indeed. You are a lovely sight, Miss Jones."

Blake wasn't too keen on the way the senator with the famously wandering eye was looking at Jennifer. "I hope you enjoyed the dinner," he said to the senator. "And made a generous donation?"

"Of course! A noble cause. We must do all we can to help

those less fortunate!"

Fearing the senator was about to launch into a speech, or try once again to recruit him into representing the party in some capacity, Blake began to plan his escape.

"Ahh, here come my son and his lovely date," the senator said, looking behind Blake. He turned to see a twenty-something man he recognized as Joshua Charles. On his arm was Elaine Sullivan. The senator made introductions all around after the couple reached them.

"A, uh … a pleasure to make your acquaintance Miss Sullivan," Blake said.

Elaine tilted her head slightly, looking at him with frank evaluation. "I was just thinking we'd met before, but I can't quite remember where."

"Well, I've been to so many of these events over the years, perhaps we've run into each other. Well, I do hope you are all enjoying yourselves. I understand we've raised more than $20,000 tonight. That will feed quite a few people. Now, if you'll excuse me, I'm afraid we do need to mingle."

"What was that all about?" Jennifer asked as he guided her away from the group. "You've spent the whole night avoiding people and now you want to mingle?"

"I just didn't want to get stuck talking to the senator. You know that he is always after me to run for something or other. I was trying to avoid having that conversation again."

Jennifer stopped and looked at him, doubt all over her face. "Uh-huh."

Blake spotted his brother and waved him over. David excused himself from his conversation and joined them.

"David, Senator Charles is here. I was thinking it would be a good idea for you to talk to him about the radio license."

"The radio … but that's your —"

Blake continued to talk over his brother. "He's here with his son and his date, Elaine Sullivan, the department store heiress.

I'm sure he won't mind if you talk a little business, though."

"Right ... of course. I'll do that."

Jennifer continued to look back and forth between the two brothers, becoming increasingly annoyed.

"You guys do realize that you are really bad at this, right? What is going on?"

"Nothing, nothing. I just ... there's nothing," Blake trailed off lamely.

Jennifer rolled her eyes at that. "Trust me, nobody's going to ask you to run for office if you can't lie any better than that. I'm going to circulate. There's got be *something* worth writing about here."

David reached out to her, but Blake grabbed his arm. "No, let her go. I told you this was a bad idea."

He glanced at his watch. "Alright, I'll make the rounds. You talk to the senator's party. We can't leave yet, but I need to stay as far away from Elaine Sullivan as possible."

An hour later, Blake was talking to the wife of the owner of Minnesota's largest pork operation. He had successfully avoided Elaine, but had noticed her looking over in his direction several times.

He felt a tap on his shoulder, and turned to see one of the hotel staff behind him.

"Excuse me, Mr. Randolph, but there is a Lt. McDaniels in the lobby. He says he must see you immediately, but he was not appropriately dressed for the dinner, so we certainly couldn't allow him ..."

"Of course, of course. I apologize Mrs. Kepler, but I do need to talk to the lieutenant."

As he left the ballroom, he saw the detective pacing back and forth across the lobby, obviously agitated. As he pivoted at one end and readied for another march across the room, he noticed Blake's approach and stopped.

"You don't look happy," Blake noted.

"Yeah, well, I was told in no uncertain terms to leave your case alone. The captain's message was that it wasn't my case and I had 'more important things to worry about.' I was not-so-subtly reminded that my high clearance rate would only get me so far if I didn't play ball."

"Jeesh, Brian, I'm sorry ..."

"Oh," McDaniels said, waving both hands in the air. "It's not like I haven't heard that before. I'm going to do my job, whether they like it or not. It really doesn't matter, though. There was nothing to find out. Nobody's investigating it. The official word is that there's nothing to see in the Gateway District. Sorry."

Blake nodded, as he hadn't really expected anything else. "I do have some more information, though, about Chicago," he said. He proceeded to fill the lieutenant in on everything he had learned on the call with Milo, including his suspicions about Detective O'Toole's death.

"That could mean something or nothing. One guy's opinion ..." the lieutenant trailed off. "Either way, there's not much more I can do for you at this point. In that regard, the captain was right ... this case isn't my job. If you find me some real evidence, something besides rumors and opinions, then maybe I can do something."

"Yes, but how many more men will disappear while you and the rest of the police are ignoring the problem?"

Blake didn't wait for an answer before pivoting away and returning to the ballroom.

VII

THE PREVIOUS evening could have gone better, Blake thought as he sat in the office that morning. The spat with Jennifer, the report from McDaniels, the close encounter with Elaine Sullivan. To top it all off, the late night had kept him from making any effort to spend time on the streets to gather more information.

Jennifer Jones wasn't in the office that morning. Rod Stanley said she had called in sick, complaining of a bad cold. So maybe he had not only screwed up his personal relationship, but also lost the paper's best reporter.

As for Elaine Sullivan, David was convinced she had no idea about Blake's dual identity. Unfortunately, he also seemed to be quite smitten with the young heiress, spending most of the ride home telling Blake how smart, beautiful and funny she was. While he had been unable to uncover much more regarding her thoughts about the Red Jackal, he had managed to ascertain that she and the senator's son were "just friends." Sometimes he forgot that David was only 23 ...

"Blake?"

Blake looked up to see Kate Gilbert standing at the door to his office.

"Sorry, Kate. Late night last night. Just woolgathering."

"Yes, I heard," she said, with a smile. "David's plan didn't go so well."

As their father's long-time assistant, the pleasant, gray-haired Kate had known both boys since they were children. Their mother died when David was a baby and Blake a teenager. Kate had been like a second mother and confidant to both boys. Blake had long suspected a relationship between his father and Kate after their mother's death, but the thought of ever asking the question horrified him. There were some things that he was better off not knowing.

"He means well, but that boy sometimes doesn't always think

things through."

"Tell me about—"

"Oh!" Kate interrupted. "Where's my head? The reception desk called up. There's an Elaine Sullivan downstairs. She's asking to see you. Isn't that the girl who was kidnapped last spring? Ellis Sullivan's daughter?"

He sighed. "Yes. Yes, it is."

"Your schedule's open until 10, but I could tell Margie you're busy if you don't want to talk to her. Send her to Rod or Frank," she said referring to the paper's top two editors.

Better to face the problem head-on, Blake decided. He wasn't going to hide from the heiress for the rest of his life. Not to mention her father was one of the paper's largest advertisers.

"No, let's see what Miss Sullivan wants from the third estate. Maybe if we're lucky she's just looking for a discount on their next advertisement."

It took only about five minutes for Elaine to make her way up to the third-floor newsroom. Blake got up from his desk to welcome her into his office.

"Good to see you again, Miss Sullivan. What can I do for you?"

"The truth is, Mr. Randolph, I had hoped to spend some more time talking to you and Miss Jones last night. I believe there is a story that the *Gazette* needs to cover. It's a story that nobody is reporting, but it's vitally important."

Elaine proceeded to describe to Blake the disappearances in the Gateway District, telling much the same story she had told the Red Jackal. Blake tried to appear as if he was hearing the information for the first time. Notably, she made no mention of the Red Jackal. Blake was happy to note she was holding to her promise to keep his alter-ego out of the papers. He was of the belief that the Red Jackal worked best as a rumor, a scary story for criminals to tell in the dark.

"Well, Miss Sullivan, this really sounds like a story for the

Minneapolis papers. I would suggest — "

Elaine cut him off. "I've already talked to them. They're not interested. The truth is I've heard that the *Gazette*, and especially Miss Jones, are more willing to write about those people who may not get much attention in the cities."

Blake held his hands up and shrugged. "I don't tell my reporters what to write about, Miss Sullivan. Miss Jones is out sick today, but if you'd like to talk to one of our other reporters … "

"I'm tired of no one caring about these people," she shouted, rising from her seat.

"I apologize," she said in a calmer voice. "But if no one official will pay attention, we will take care of this ourselves. I've already taken … well, that's unimportant."

"That's a dangerous game to play, Miss Sullivan."

"Yes," she said, looking more closely at Blake. "I suppose it is. Mr. Randolph, do you — "

"Elaine! I heard you were here!"

Both Elaine and Blake looked to the doorway in response to David's voice.

"Hello, David," she said, giving the younger Randolph brother a much nicer look than the elder.

"Blake, Kate asked me to remind you about your appointment at the brickyard."

"Oh, yes, I do have to go," Blake said looking at his watch. "Miss Sullivan, maybe we can continue this conversation at another date."

David turned his attention back to Elaine. "I'd be happy to show you out. I realize it's a little early for lunch, but perhaps a cup of coffee. The shop in the lobby is quite good."

Elaine glanced back at Blake before agreeing.

"Have a good meeting, Blake," David said as he guided Elaine out of the office, ignoring Blake's warning look.

VIII

THE RED Jackal was back in the Gateway District as the setting sun reflected off the Mississippi River. He had spent the last two hours carefully moving from rooftop to rooftop, quietly watching the comings and goings of Skid Row.

He had observed the usual petty crimes and misdemeanors, but nothing that shone any light on the disappearances. It was clear a more active approach was needed.

A silent vibration from his wrist alerted the Jackal to an incoming message from Geoffrey. Thanks to a helpful contact in the Canadian government, Geoffrey had recently acquired two-way radio technology that had drastically improved the ability of the Jackal to communicate when he was out on the town. Radio receivers in the car, his office and his home – not to mention his new wrist radio – made him reachable almost anywhere.

"Go ahead, Geoffrey," he said, speaking into the small wireless device.

"Yes, sir. Miss Sullivan just called. She said she needs to see you right away at the mission. She sounded quite distraught."

"Thank you, Geoffrey. I'm only minutes away."

"Quite good, sir. She said to come to the back door off the alley and she'll let you in where you can escape notice."

The Jackal, quickly leaping from building to building, arrived at the mission within minutes. He dropped quietly to the ground after observing that the alley was empty. He rapped once on the dented steel door, which was opened by Elaine within seconds.

"In here," she whispered, pulling the Jackal through the doorway. "This way," she said, indicating a narrow hallway. Twenty feet down the hall she opened a door to what appeared to be a janitor's closet, with mops, brooms, dustpans and other cleaning supplies scattered about in front of a large slop sink.

"What's this about?" the masked vigilante said, hoping the deeper voice he used in his guise as the Jackal would keep Elaine from recognizing him.

"Ernie's disappeared. I think he's been taken."

Elaine went on to explain that Ernie hadn't shown up for his shift that morning at the mission. He had helped clean the floors after dinner the previous evening and then told Sister Katherine he was walking home, leaving about 9 p.m. Elaine and Sister Katherine had visited his rooming house this afternoon and found that nobody there had seen him since he left for the mission the night before.

"Some of the men here ... well, I would think they went off a drinking binge, but not Ernie. This job was so important to him. I just know something's happened!"

"I'm inclined to believe you. I'm a good judge of character and my impression of Ernie is that he is on the path to restoring his life. Now, where is this rooming house? I want to —"

He paused as he heard a barely audible scraping sound outside the door. He could see shifting shadows through the gap between the door and floor.

" — talk to some of the people who live there."

"Keep talking," he whispered to Elaine, as he quietly moved to the door.

Elaine was clearly confused by the request, but complied.

"Of course, uh, we can go talk to them as soon as you want so you can find out ... so you can find out what you need to know. I think we can go over there tonight if you want ..."

The Jackal opened the door with his left hand and reached out with his right hand, grabbing their listener. Lifting the dirt-smeared man a foot off the ground, he slammed the door shut with his leg. He realized it was Gerald, once again making an appearance. The man looked as frightened as he did two nights earlier in the alley.

"Why were you listening to us?" the Jackal asked in his deepest, most menacing voice, the voice that reduced criminals throughout the Twin Cities to a quivering mass. With his back to

Elaine, only Gerald could see his eyes briefly take on a reddish glow – another invention of Geoffrey's.

"Don't hurt me!" Gerald wailed. "I'll tell you whatever you want to know. Don't hurt me!"

The Jackal dropped the man to the floor, where he collapsed in a whimpering heap.

"What are you doing?" Elaine shouted at the Jackal, grabbing his arm and spinning him around.

"This man," he said with disdain in his voice, "knows much more than he is telling you. He was in the mission when I talked to Ernie yesterday."

Elaine raised her voice to match the Jackal's tone. "Wait, that doesn't mean he's guilty of anything!"

"Why don't you ask him why he had this in the alley Wednesday night?" The Jackal held up the pistol he had seen Gerald discard as he ran out of the alley.

"Gerald? I said no weapons … I didn't want anyone to get hurt! What were you thinking?"

"He knows where Ernie is … and if you want to find him alive, we don't have time to waste on niceties!"

The Jackal turned back to the cowering man. "Tell her the truth!"

"I'm sorry! They said no one was going to get hurt … and then it was too late … I liked Ernie … I didn't …"

"What?" Elaine said, as she collapsed into the only chair in the room, her open mouth and wet eyes reflecting the crushing realization that Gerald *was* involved.

It took only a few minutes for the Jackal to collect the basic facts. Gerald had been approached by a "high-class guy" several weeks earlier who claimed to be a doctor, looking for men to hire for an important job. All Gerald had to do was help him find some strong men, men who were willing to work. It was secret work, so it had to be kept very quiet. In exchange Gerald got plenty of Canadian whiskey and a promise of a large cash payment. Later, another man, who sounded to the Jackal like the man Ernie had seen with Cap, showed up as well.

It didn't take long for Gerald to realize that the first three men he recommended never showed up again at the mission. When he asked the doctor about that, the promises turned to threats. Who would the authorities believe, he asked Gerald, a respected doctor or a skid row bum? The three men were dead and a call to the police would tie Gerald to their murders, he said.

After that, the Jackal saw, it was a simple case of manipulating Gerald to help them capture more men for whatever this work was. Gerald was also told to keep an eye out for any interest in the disappearances. When he told them of Elaine's plan to contact the Red Jackal, they provided him with a gun and Gerald was told to try to kill both of them, as well as Ernie and Kurt, and make it look like a mugging gone bad. Faced with the Jackal in person, though, he had lost his nerve. It was fairly clear to the Jackal that the plan was designed to make sure Gerald was killed or caught himself.

Gerald had never recommended Ernie for the "job" despite his obvious strength, because, as he said, he liked him. But he talked to Ernie after he observed the meeting, and discovered the stranger was the Red Jackal. When he reported that to the doctor, he was told to arrange a meeting with Ernie.

Thursday night he waited in the doorway of a shuttered bar that he knew was on the route between the mission and Ernie's rooming house. It was easy enough to get the man to follow him into the adjacent bakery when he said he had found something out about the disappearances. The doctor and the other man were waiting for them there with guns drawn. They took Ernie and told Gerald to watch for any interest in Ernie's disappearance. He was also supposed to bring the men another test subject tonight.

"I didn't have a choice," Gerald sobbed.

"There's always a choice," the Jackal said, looking at the wretched man with a combination of pity and disgust. "And now you have another chance to make the right one. You're going to help us find these men and stop them."

IX

THE NEXT two hours were a flurry of activity. The Jackal raced away from the mission to the hidden Packard where he quickly remade his face and appearance in the guise of a down-on-his-luck individual. His mastery of costumes and disguise ensured that even someone who knew Blake Randolph would not recognize him. From Elaine he had acquired some discarded clothing that had been found in a back room.

From the privacy of the sedan, he contacted Geoffrey and ordered him to drive to an alley down the street from the mission. He was waiting there when Geoffrey arrived and quickly detailed his plan to let himself be captured. He explained Gerald's involvement to ensure that if something happened to him the man would still be held responsible for his actions. He also charged him with watching over Miss Sullivan, who had refused to leave the mission.

"It's our best way to stop these men, Geoffrey," he said to his dubious driver. "If you don't hear from me by tomorrow morning, talk to David. Until then, this stays between us."

"As you wish, sir," Geoffrey reluctantly agreed.

Once back at the mission, he went over the plan again with Gerald, realizing that he was trusting its success to a man who had proven himself to be anything but trustworthy. Gerald was supposed to deliver the latest volunteer to the bakery at 10 p.m. That gave them less than 15 minutes, just enough time to reach the location. If the criminals followed their usual pattern, they would send Gerald away when they departed with the latest "worker."

"Don't think about double-crossing me, Gerald. Miss Sullivan knows about you. My associates know about you. If anything happens to me, they'll come for you."

"I know, I know. I just want to get this over with."

"Then let's go," the Jackal said as the two men stepped through the doorway.

Within minutes they reached the closed bakery. Gerald knocked on the door – once, twice, once – and a balding man in glasses answered. He stood about six inches shorter than the Jackal's normal height, although he was purposely slouching over in his guise as a derelict this night.

"Come on in, Gerald!" the man said with a friendly, broad smile. "And who's your friend?"

"Uh, this is Jimmy, Doc."

The doctor continued to project an aura of happiness to his guests.

"Great! Jimmy, so glad you could come and see us. I am Dr. Stone and this is my partner Maxwell," he said gesturing toward a nattily attired, thin, mustachioed man with dark hair. Cleary the mysterious "well-dressed" man Ernie had seen with Cap before he was taken.

"I'm sure Gerald's told you that we have a job for you," the doctor continued. "We're going to be reopening this bakery in a few weeks and as you can see we've got a lot of work to do.

"Tonight, I need you to come to our warehouse with us to help load up some equipment we need over here. Then we'll need some help cleaning this place. You do a good job tonight and we'll have a job for you the rest of the week – maybe even longer. We'll pay you $5 tonight and $2 a day the rest of the week. How's that sound to you?"

The man was a persuasive salesman, the Jackal had to give him that. It was clear why it had been so easy to find recruits. For men living on handouts and what they could beg off the street, $5 was a veritable fortune.

"Yes, sir. Sounds mighty fair."

"Wonderful, wonderful." *That smile is really starting to get on my nerves,* the Jackal thought.

With that, the doctor quickly dismissed Gerald, who slunk out the front door with his new bottle of whiskey. He and Maxwell took "Jimmy" out the back door, and guided him to the green delivery truck parked in the alley behind the bakery, "Meadowlark Bread" painted on the side.

"You're gonna have to ride in back," Maxwell said with a snarl. "There's no room for you in front." He shoved the Jackal toward the open back door of the truck. He pulled himself into the box, grunting with effort to hide the ease of the move. As soon as he cleared the deck, Maxwell slammed the doors shut.

The Jackal stood facing the door until the truck started to move, then sat on the floor of the box. The ride was a bumpy but short one – less than 10 minutes – so they were almost certainly still in the general area of the Gateway District. As the truck slowed, he rose to his feet again, ready to react to whatever was on the other side of those doors.

The doors suddenly flew open to show a brightly lit warehouse, briefly blinding him. The smell of the Mississippi told him they were near the water.

"Get down and get over here," Maxwell said, pointing a .38 at him. He climbed down slowly, still playing the part of the tramp.

"Huh? What? What's with the gun, mister?"

"I said get over here!"

"Yeah, sure, whatever you say." The Jackal began to slowly move toward Maxwell and Dr. Stone, now standing about 10 feet away. He mentally prepared himself to strike.

Dr. Stone smiled again, but this time there was no friendliness in the predatory grin. "Little change of plans, Jimmy. I'm afraid you're not going to get that $5, but I do have a very important job for you."

The Jackal looked around the large, open room in which they had parked the truck and saw no sign of Ernie – or anyone else for that matter. Deciding it was time to get answers, he sprung at Maxwell. A quick blow to his right hand sent the gun flying. The Jackal spun, catching the .38 in midair, and delivering a kick that sent Maxwell flying into a steel pillar. He slumped to the floor, unmoving.

The Jackal aimed his newly acquired pistol at the doctor, who stood, stunned, in front of him.

"Thanks for the invite, Doc, but I'm changing those plans again. Let's talk about what's going on here."

He saw a brief flicker of the doctor's eyes, but the warning came too late. He felt a sting in the back of his leg, then nothing as he slipped into the darkness.

X

THE JACKAL awoke to a faceful of water, his head pounding.

"Wakey, wakey!" he heard the voice of Dr. Stone say through the cobwebs in his head. The headache and cloudy feeling told him he had been drugged; an injection of some sort would explain the sting he remembered.

He opened his eyes to see Dr. Stone about three feet in front of him; behind him a stooped, shriveled man in a wheelchair sat holding what appeared to be a modified pistol of some sort. There was something vaguely familiar about his face, but the Jackal couldn't place it.

The Jackal was sitting on a wooden chair, his hands bound behind him. He saw he was in some sort of laboratory, but a spacious one measuring at least 100 feet by 100 feet. To his right was a set-up that looked like something out of an apothecary: various liquids, canisters of powders, test tubes, mortar and pestle. A steel bookcase stood next to it. To his left, a table with straps on it, clearly designed to hold a patient – or victim – in place. Directly in front of him was a steel door that seemed likely to lead out to the larger warehouse.

"Enough, he's awake," the wheelchair-bound man snapped. "So, you must be the famous Red Jackal. Hmmm, seems we had little to worry about. Well, most of us. Maxwell might disagree! It's a good thing for you I hated that nephew of mine.

"He had been waiting years for me to die and I still outlived him! Hee hee!"

The Jackal shook his head and blinked his eyes, trying to clear his head.

"Feeling a little sleepy? You can thank Dr. Stone for that. This dart gun is a little something he whipped up to control our more … unruly patients. It uses a special concoction of his to take down even the strongest man, something that proves quite useful, I must say." He laughed, sounding to the Jackal like Dwight Frye in a Universal horror pic. "You're going to get to see that yourself!"

As the man talked, the Jackal had continued to feel around the chair behind his back. When he discovered a sharp edge sticking out of the frame, he jammed his left arm into it. The pain cleared the last of the fogginess even as he could feel the blood running down his wrist. He knew that the longer he could keep the men talking, the better.

"So let's make sure we're all up to speed here. You're killing men from the streets; men you thought no one would miss. You did the same thing in Chicago several years ago. Clearly, you're doing some sort of experiment on these men. I'm going to guess it has something to do with that wheelchair you're in."

The look on Dr. Stone's face said he was surprised by the depth of the knowledge, but his associate only smiled, chuckling quietly.

"Very impressive! It seems you're not a complete idiot, but you got some of it wrong."

"Well, why don't you enlighten me," the Jackal said, as he tried to surreptitiously move his hands to weaken the rope on the sharp edge.

"Why not? Doctor, why don't you go make sure our next experiment is ready for our guest?" He paused as the doctor opened the heavy steel door and exited into the dark hallway beyond. The door clanged shut behind him.

"Where was I? Oh, yes. You were quite right about my condition. Nobody has been able to determine exactly what is wrong with me. I spent thousands of dollars with some of the world's greatest doctors, but no one was able to figure out why I seemed to be wasting away … until I found Dr. Wright. He developed a formula that reversed my deterioration, but it took quite a bit of experimentation to get it right. Luckily, there were plenty of test subjects available in Chicago."

"Test subjects? They were men …"

"They were refuse, drags on society," he snarled. "At least this way they served some purpose, by restoring the life of an important man, a builder, a creator of industry, a —"

The Jackal suddenly realized why he recognized the man. "Henry Howard," he said.

"Ha ha, yes. I suppose the face is still recognizable, even as the body has failed me."

Henry Howard was one of the wealthiest men in America, owner of everything from mining interests to banks to factories. He was also one of American's most famous recluses, having disappeared from the public eye nearly a decade ago.

Howard wheeled closer to the Jackal's chair, warily watching the man.

"Now you see why it's so important that I am healthy! Thousands of hard-working men depend on me for their livelihood! I am more important than any simple man!"

The man's not just a narcissist, but certifiably insane.

"Dr. Wright found the cure and restored me to full health. Unfortunately, the fix turned out to be a temporary one. After a few years, my body started to fail me again. I had made the admittedly ill-advised decision to kill Dr. Wright after his discovery – he simply knew too much.

"That's where Dr. Stone comes in. He was a disgraced man, an abortionist who failed to safely perform the procedure on the daughter of the wrong man – but still a genius with medicine, engineering, electronics. It took him a while, but he had Dr. Wright's notes. Just a few days ago, I could barely breathe on my own. Tonight, I can talk to you without losing my breath. I'll be walking again soon!

"Anyone who takes this formula becomes exponentially stronger and healthier!"

The Jackal had almost worked his hands free. *Only a little longer, just keep him talking.*

"But why here? Why come to Minneapolis?"

"Oh, it was convenient. Every city has a skid row, men who will do anything for a promise of money. It seemed unlikely we'd be caught in Chicago, but why take the chance on doing it again? There was one detective who stumbled on to our experiments, but it was easy to take care of him. Still, Dr. Stone preferred to leave the bad publicity of his failure behind.

"I admittedly did not anticipate anyone catching on so quickly here, but we'll take care of that shortly. I assume I've given you almost enough time to work free by now, so I will take my leave. Feel free to leave the laboratory as soon as you finish up back there."

Howard pressed a button on his chair and the door opened behind him. He flew backward in his electric chair, turning his back on the Jackal only as he reached the doorway. The steel door slammed shut behind him.

What the hell do they have planned?

With no other ideas readily apparent, the Jackal continued to work on the rope. No longer trying to hide his efforts it took only a few minutes to cut through the bindings. He stood up and rubbed his wrists to restore the feeling in his hands and began looking around the lab for a weapon of some sort.

His first thought was to try the table, but if there had been any surgical tools in the room, they were gone now. He swiftly moved to the other side of the room and began looking at the chemicals and mixtures there.

"Nothing's labeled," he muttered in frustration, looking at the two bottles in his hand, one filled with yellow powder; the other a clear liquid. The door slammed open at that moment, and the lights in the laboratory went out, plunging him into darkness.

Suddenly, lights lit up the long hallway. The Jackal stuffed the two bottles into his pockets, then slowly moved across the lab toward the light and stepped into the passageway.

XI

THE HALLWAY was about 200 feet long, with what appeared to be offices, storage rooms, even a bathroom, on either side. The Jackal tensed, ready for a surprise from any direction.

Instead, the surprise was that he made it down the hallway with no attacks. He reached the end of the hall, and cautiously stepped into the same large warehouse space in which he had first arrived.

"Welcome to your doom, Red Jackal!" It was Howard, speaking from an elevated walkway that ringed most of the main room, some 15 feet above floor level. Dr. Stone stood nearby.

"I promised that you would get to take part in one last experiment."

The Jackal quickly surveyed the room and saw that there appeared to be only two ways to reach the walkway: either via a set of stairs hundreds of yards away, across the warehouse, or the hydraulic elevator just 20 feet away, but raised to the upper level.

"As it turns out," Howard continued, "Dr. Stone made another discovery during his experimentation – a compound that makes those who take it mindless automatons. Combining both formulas ... well, I don't know how I'll use that yet, but with Dr.

Stone's mind and my money, there will be little we can't do!"

"Stone! You know what he did to his last doctor – you can't trust him!"

"Nice try, Jackal. Dr. Stone and I have an understanding. He gives me power; I support his lifestyle. Without me he might as well be dead."

With a running start, I might be able to leap to reach that walkway and pull myself up. With that thought in mind, he started slowly backing away toward where the truck was still parked.

"Fine, Howard, what's this experiment of yours? Stop talking and get to it!"

Howard smiled, seemingly almost giddy with the excitement. "Simple. I spoke of combining the formulas – we did just that with our latest patient. Ernie, time to come out and play!" he said as he clapped his hands.

The Jackal heard a *thump* behind him and whirled to see Ernie, who had just emerged from the back of the truck. The boxer had not only been restored to his former heavyweight glory, but looked like he might be even stronger than when Blake had seem him fight more than decade earlier. The Jackal started to walk slowly toward Ernie.

"Ernie – it's me. The Red Jackal – Miss Sullivan's friend. You don't want to hurt me. I'm here to help."

"Kill him!" Howard yelled. Ernie nodded once and charged the Red Jackal. His first blow sent the Jackal flying back almost 20 feet. He flipped himself at the last moment to avoid landing fully on the concrete floor.

"You want to stop him, you have to kill him, Jackal!" Howard said, chortling.

He was determined to do that only as a last resort. He knew Ernie was not acting of his own volition. The Jackal sprung to his feet, ready to meet the attacking Ernie. *Another direct hit like that might finish me.*

This time, as Ernie swung, he leaped over the giant's back,

delivering a blow to the back of his neck. He hit solid muscle. A move that would have normally stunned any fighter resulted in nothing but a sore hand for the Jackal. *He may be stronger, but I'm still faster.*

The Jackal sprinted for the empty truck, hearing Ernie giving chase behind him. He purposely slowed as he approached the truck, allowing the boxer to end up only a few paces behind. He heard Ernie launch toward him and slid under the truck. He heard the crash and then a bellow of pain and anger as Ernie slammed into the truck, missing the Jackal by inches. He rolled through to the other side as the truck rocked on its wheels.

Ernie screamed in anger, then began pushing on the side of the truck. The Jackal looked up to see the truck beginning to tilt over. *This is not good.* He scrambled away, narrowly escaping as the truck crashed over on its side.

The truck had proven to be little obstacle for the fighter. Although bloodied and bruised, he seemed undeterred. Ernie had jumped onto the now toppled truck and was preparing to leap down to the floor where the Jackal lay. The Jackal rolled again as Ernie attacked, then sprung to his feet.

Moving toward the front of the truck, he spotted the bumper, now laying on the ground. He grabbed it, swinging it at Ernie in one move. He connected with his head, stunning Ernie momentarily. He prepared for a second swing, only to have Ernie grab the other end and rip it from his hands. The Jackal looked desperately around the warehouse for additional weapons, but the empty space offered little in way of solutions. *Time for another idea.*

The Jackal moved back toward Howard and the doctor, stopping just short of the walkway, knowing he had to time his next move just right. As Ernie approached and prepared to swing at him, the Jackal grabbed his arm and flipped over the giant's head, landing directly behind him. As Ernie spun around, the Jackal reached into his pocket, tossing the powdered contents of one of the containers in the fighter's eyes. *Sorry, Ernie. Hope that doesn't cause permanent damage.*

Ernie grabbed his face, yelling in pain. The Jackal leaped onto the man's shoulders, using them as a springboard to reach the elevated walkway. Howard tried to raise the dart gun in his direction, but the Jackal knocked it to the steel grating before he could fire. He followed that up with a kick that sent the industrialist's wheelchair spinning away.

A bullet pinged off the railing, just short of the Jackal.

"Turn around!" The Jackal slowly turned to see Dr. Stone holding what appeared to be the departed Maxwell's .38. The twitching of his eyes and unsteadiness of his hand told the Jackal that Stone was unused to handling firearms.

"Enough of these games. Howard has had his fun."

As the doctor talked, the Jackal surreptitiously removed the cork from the vial of liquid he had removed from the laboratory. Watching the doctor, he saw his finger being to tighten on the trigger and threw the clear liquid directly at his face. Dr. Stone dropped the gun and screamed as the skin began to smoke. "It burns ..." he gurgled, falling to his knees.

He pivoted to deal with Howard, but at the same time, felt a steel grip on his left leg and looked down to see Ernie hanging from the latticed steel. With one swift move, he pulled the Jackal from the walkway and threw him to the floor. His head slammed into the concrete, momentarily stunning him.

Before he could regain his feet, Ernie had delivered a punch to his chest. The pain he felt when he gasped for air told him the blow had broken at least one rib. The Jackal pushed himself up, dodging the next punch, then another. Moving more quickly than he thought possible, Ernie reached out and grabbed the Jackal by the shoulders and lifted him over his head. He tossed the vigilante against the sheet metal wall of the warehouse, 20 yards away, as if he weighed next to nothing.

Seeing stars, the Jackal tried to stand, but collapsed as his injured leg gave out beneath him.

"Wait!" he heard Howard shout from the walkway.

The Jackal heard the *whir* of the elevator as Howard lowered himself to the ground level, then wheeled over next to Ernie.

"Jackal, I'll give you one last chance," Howard said. "You can come work for me. Just think what this formula can do for a man like you. Power, wealth beyond belief. It appears I'll have an opening to replace the good doctor, someone to run my empire."

"Not ... a ... chance," the Jackal gasped through clenched teeth, pushing himself up against the wall, fighting to a standing position.

"Finish him!" Howard ordered Ernie.

Ernie had taken just one step toward the Jackal when a gunshot rang out. Ernie grabbed his arm, blood running out between his fingers. The Jackal looked up to see Lt. McDaniels slide to the floor, having entered through a broken window. He set his feet, preparing for a second shot.

"No!" the Jackal yelled, grabbing his arm just as he fired, causing the shot to go wide. It flew past Ernie, hitting Howard's oxygen tank. Howard was engulfed in the sudden explosion and the shockwave sent Ernie flying across the room. The flash temporarily blinded the Jackal and his friend.

"What the hell were you doing?" McDaniels asked.

"That man was one of the kidnapped men. He was drugged, out of his mind. It wasn't his fault."

"Hmmm," McDaniels responded doubtfully as he carefully approached the fallen boxer. "Well, he's breathing, but he's out cold. If he wakes up again, I'm not promising I won't shoot him.

"This guy," he said, walking toward the melted remains of the wheelchair, "is well-done. Anybody else I should be worried about?"

"Yeah, there's a doctor. He should be up on that walkway. I threw some sort of acid in his face."

The lieutenant found no sign of the doctor there; the Jackal directed him to the laboratory, thinking he might have tried to hide there. That search proved fruitless as well.

"We've got to get you out of here," McDaniels said. "Even in this neighborhood an explosion and gunshots won't be ignored for too long. I have to call this in and I'd rather not explain the presence of the Red Jackal."

The Jackal rose slowly, using a broken board as a crutch.

"Wait a minute," he said. "What are you doing here? I thought you said you weren't going to be able to help."

McDaniels smiled. "What do you think? Geoffrey decided to make an executive decision and ignore your directions. When he called told me about your idiotic plan, I knew you were going to need me to bail you out. Luckily, I had time to get near that bakery and follow you when you left. The only problem was they made some quick turns down here and I didn't know exactly which building you were in. There's about a dozen old factories and warehouses in a row here. I'm just glad I made it in time."

The Jackal winced as he hobbled toward the door. "Not a problem. I had everything under control."

Blake Randolph was sitting propped up in bed when Geoffrey announced that he had a visitor the next afternoon.

"Tsk, tsk, tsk. I can't believe you totaled the Roadster. I think we should be taking away your license, young man," McDaniels said as her walked into the bedroom.

"Very funny." A car accident had seemed the best explanation for Blake's injuries. Geoffrey, who had been waiting with the Packard near the warehouse, had driven him to the Randolph estate, where a discreet doctor had examined him. He had two broken ribs, a severely sprained ankle, a probable concussion, and countless bruises and scrapes.

"You'll be happy to know your friend Ernie woke up about an hour ago," McDaniels said. "We had him shackled, but it doesn't look like that will be necessary for long. Whatever we saw last night seems to have worn off. He says he doesn't remember much of anything after he was taken."

"What's going to happen to him?"

"Luckily, there are a lot of people who want this covered up. The brass doesn't want the citizens of Minneapolis to know they missed a murderer picking off people right under their noses. Then this morning some G-Men showed up, emptied out the lab and left. They took everything – the books, notes, chemicals. The point is, nobody seems real interested in Ernie. They're willing to chalk him up as a victim and close the case."

"What about Dr. Stone?"

"Oh, here's where things get especially interesting: Did you notice that bookcase in the lab? Well, it was on sliders and behind it was a tunnel and a safe. The safe was empty, but I followed the tunnel and eventually came out on the other side of the block. I have to assume that's what happened to your Dr. Stone.

"But officially, he doesn't exist," McDaniels said. "After all, you were never there and I never saw him. A third killer would only complicate things, my friend."

Epilogue

The hooded man, his face a stiff mask, hurried down the street. He looked at his feet as he moved, rarely glancing up, dodging light and avoiding any interaction until he reached the dark stairway.

He quickly looked up and down the street, then scurried down the stairs to the basement.

His inner sanctum was dark, filled with shadows. The only illumination was what street light bled in through the small hopper window over his head.

But that meant nothing to the man sitting at the small table facing the wall. Light no longer mattered to him.

He slowly pulled down his hood, then removed the black wig covering his scarred, bald head. Finally, off came the faceplate, a complicated device with hooks and wires. That revealed his true face – a blank, featureless canvas that would have horrified anyone who saw it. As his right hand brushed his face, his left slammed the table in mute rage, but he quickly calmed himself.

He had time. He had money. He had intelligence. That was all a man needed to wreak vengeance.

A Tip of the Cowl

The Gateway District, site of the kidnappings and experiments in this story did and does currently exist, although it now bears little resemblance to its long history as Minneapolis's skid row.

First known as "Bridge Square," it was the original downtown of Minneapolis due to its location near the Mississippi River. As the center of the city shifted as Minneapolis grew, the area became the site of boarding houses, saloons, bordellos and other questionable establishments.

By the 1900s, the area had become firmly entrenched as the home of a mostly male, poor, transient population. The Great Depression only furthered that.

Various renewal efforts by city leaders over the years proved unsuccessful – including its rebranding as the Gateway District, complete with a new park. It wasn't until the Federal Highway Act of 1956 and the construction of the interstate system that the Gateway District ceased to exist as it had been known for decades.

For better or worse, most of the neighborhood and hundreds of buildings were razed during the late 1950s and 1960s. Among the demolished buildings was the Metropolitan, the city's first skyscraper.

As for the kidnappings and experiments conducted by Dr. Stone and Henry Howard, those are purely a figment of the author's imagination.

RED JACKAL

BORN

The Red Jackal uncovers the secrets of ancient Egypt!

My earlier recountings of the Red Jackal's adventures have been based on the writings and somewhat polished stories left behind by my uncle. The story told here, on the other hand, seems to have never been completed.

I found it in a box labeled, simply, "Egypt." I can only assume it was part of an aborted effort to tell the story of the origin of the Red Jackal. The majority of the record is made up of a contemporary journal, but also telegrams, newspaper articles and some writings that seem to have been completed at a later date.

Clearly, countless hours were spent on the accumulation of these recordings and writings, but whether for lack of time or interest, the project was never completed. Even if only for historical purposes, it seems important to include in the chronicling of his adventures.

Where necessary, I have interjected some notes for context. – DR

Brickton Gazette
September 10, 1922
Blake Randolph joins Egypt expedition

Local war hero Blake Randolph announced today he will be joining the forthcoming expedition of renowned Egyptologist Dr. James Prowse of the British Museum.

Randolph is the son of Ludlow Randolph, publisher of this paper and mayor of our fine city. Blake Randolph only recently returned from Europe, where he received the Distinguished Service Cross for his service on the Western Front. Since the cessation of hostilities, Mr. Randolph has served ably as an attaché at the U.S. Embassy in London.

Randolph tells us that it was in his time there that he met Dr. Prowse, widely considered one of the great minds in the field of archeology. Dr. Prowse is preparing to undertake a new exploration in the Egyptian desert. The great doctor is said to have a specific goal in mind, but in a telegram to our correspondent only would say that he believes he is on the cusp of a "great discovery." We are led to understand that secrecy such as that is common in the field, as there is always the danger of another team "poaching" a discovery.

Randolph will depart next week via train to New York, where he will board the RMS Humphrey, which will take him on his journey to Alexandria.

September 16, 1922
Letter of Blake Randolph to Miss Jennifer Jones

Dear Jennifer,

Thank you for the kind gift of the journal. As you suggested in your note, it will be a wonderful way to chronicle this adventure. You truly have a way with words that will serve you well at the university this fall. I am so very proud of you, as I know Eddie would be as well.

Yours,

Blake

September 18, 1922
Entry in Journal of Blake Randolph

I have always felt more comfortable on the business side of our family enterprises than the journalistic side, and never have been one to put my thoughts to paper. Perhaps this gift from Jennifer will be an inspiration. It was quite a shock to see her again after all these years, no longer the 12-year-old girl that Eddie and I left in Brickton five years ago. I imagine she will find herself with no shortage of suitors in the fall ...

Time to sleep. The ship departs at sunrise tomorrow.

POTENTIAL TROUBLE WITH EXPEDITION. DELAY
DEPARTURE IF POSSIBLE.

Boarded the ship without incident. Relatively small contingent of passengers, I'm told, with only about 400 on board including the crew. We will be picking up more passengers at stops in the Azores and Gibraltar before making our way to Alexandria.

Dined tonight with Capt. Powell, a veteran of the British Navy. At least we are in good hands. Joining us at the captain's table were Victor Wadsworth, son of the vessel's owner, and his new wife. They recently embarked on a world tour for their honeymoon, having sailed to New York last month and now continuing on their way.

I ended up seated next to a Mr. Bradley, a rather annoying Englishman. He says he is returning to Cairo, where he has lived since before the war. Once he found out I was going to be working with Dr. Prowse, he could hardly contain himself. He is a student of the pyramids who seems to travel with his own library. He is also apparently an occasional correspondent with the *Egypt News & Mail*, which he tells me is Egypt's oldest English-language newspaper, and has been very excited to tell me more than I could ever want to know about the history of the land.

A most unusual occurrence this evening. I was dining with the captain as has been my wont during the trip thus far. After dinner, I made my exit to avoid another conversation with Bradley, who seems determined to befriend me on this voyage.

I was walking the upper deck of the ship when a young woman of incredible beauty materialized out of the crowd. She had an olive complexion reminiscent of the Mediterranean, and dark, pure black hair, but spoke English in the precise manner of a citizen of the crown.

"Mr. Blake Randolph, the American." she stated more than asked. I still responded in the affirmative.

"We are told you are a good man, a man of character, a hero, as it were," she said. "A man who has shown great bravery in the past and will again."

I was admittedly confused, and embarrassed by the characterization. "We? If you refer to my service in the war, it was nothing that thousands of other men didn't do."

"We are known by many names, but most know us as the Kenk. We have hope for you, but also fear," she continued. "Being a brave man will not ensure your survival."

"Survival? Survival of what?"

"Of what is to come. Your strength of character has earned you this warning. There is still time to abandon the expedition, to return to your land, and leave the master undisturbed."

Understanding dawned! This woman was clearly one of those native Egyptians who resent the unearthing of the tombs of the pharaohs and was trying to dissuade me from the effort.

"Let me assure you, Dr. Prowse is one of the – "

"He is not worthy of our concern. You are," she said briefly touching my face, then stepping back into the crowd before I could even respond.

I quickly shook off my stupor, and attempted to follow her

but was stopped by Mr. Bradley. By the time I could extricate myself from that conversation, the young woman was nowhere to be seen.

As the hour was late, I have retired to my cabin. Tomorrow I shall endeavor to find this woman.

September 22, 1922
Entry in Journal of Blake Randolph

Yesterday's odd occurrence gets odder. I find no trace of my strange visitor. None of the crew recognized my description and the relatively small passenger list makes it unlikely she could have escaped notice.

The mate posits that she may be spending her time in the cabin. Says there are several passengers who do that on every crossing, but does admit that if she is as beautiful as I say, she would likely be remembered by somebody.

September 26, 1922
Entry in Journal of Blake Randolph

Of all the luck! Ol' Douglas Morrow has joined the ship during our brief stop in the Azores. Have not seen him since we parted ways in France more than three years ago. He has been enjoying life as a "wandering adventurer" since then. He tells me that despite his father's passing, his mother still resides in Brussels, but that he finds his brief returns to the continent to be "quite tedious."

He was entertaining me with his tales of Africa and the Mediterranean. He recently had, as he put it, an "unfortunate misunderstanding" involving the daughter of an important merchant in the Azores prompting his quick departure. I imagine it was like some of those "unfortunate misunderstandings" he managed to get himself into with many a French girl!

We stayed up quite late recounting our tales of glory during the war. I'm sure the captain will be quite happy to have Douglas join us at his table tomorrow night.

Mother,

I write you from the RMS Humphrey en route to Alexandria, Egypt. My stay in the Azores was cut short by bad weather.

You will be pleased to know that I encountered my old friend Blake Randolph on board. I know how much you enjoyed talking to him when we visited after the war ended. He sends his best. Blake is making his way to Alexandria as well to join in an expedition with Dr. James Prowse, the renowned British Egyptologist. They are involved in a search of some sort, but it's all very hush-hush.

With my recent change in plans, I may see about joining the effort.

I know you worry about me, mother, and my wandering ways. I fear that I still find myself seeking some purpose in life. In the War, I was fighting for the greater good. Oh, to have a mission again! Perhaps this Egypt trip will offer some excitement.

I will endeavor to keep you better informed of where I venture next and will try to make it back to Brussels shortly.

Your Loving Son,
Douglas

After breakfast this morning, I shared my mysterious encounter with Douglas, jesting that my misunderstandings never end as well as his! Was surprised by his reaction: "This is nothing to joke about, my friend. I have been to that land; you have not. If I have learned anything over these last few years it is that we in the West have a poor understanding of those things that remain unseen."

I am severely disappointed in Douglas; afraid we parted on rough terms.

I am a man of science and business, not one to believe in superstitious folly. There is a terrestrial explanation for this, I am sure. Douglas has spent too much time chasing fair maidens in the sun. If I am in danger, it is of the man-made sort. There is certainly evil in the world, but it is all too secular. The Western Front taught me that. Man needs no help in that regard.

(later)

Dinner took a maddening turn. Despite my protestations, Douglas once again brought the subject up for discussion. Mr. Bradley had joined us at the captain's table as has been his pattern and overheard our disagreement, me on the side of science, Douglas on the side of superstition.

"'Ah, it is the fault of our science that it wants to explain all; and if it explain not, then it says there is nothing to explain,'" Bradley offered.

He asked what was prompting our battle. As we explained the situation to him, a strange gleam came into his eye. "I believe I have a book that may shed some light on this debate. I consider myself a man of science, but your description of events … well, as I said, this tome may provide, if not answers, at least some basis for further discussion. I doubt there is a supernatural explanation, but this does make for an interesting note. What say we return at 8 o'clock for brandy?"

Douglas and I answered in the affirmative; both hoping to put the discussion to rest, I'm sure. It is almost time to return to the dining room, so more later.

(evening)

Have Bradley's book. He has shown us a painting of an Egyptian Oracle of sorts that could be of the woman I met … or any other attractive Egyptian woman in her twenties. Hardly conclusive proof. I will at least read up on her and humor these two men.

Excerpt from "Egypt: Her People and Myths" by William Benedict

… Little is known of the history of the cult of Kenk today. What survives in myth is a story of a cult made up entirely of women, a group of priestesses said to wield great power in their quest to serve and protect the spiritual leader Kentenkamen.

Even less is known of Kentenkamen, who history records appearing in Egypt sometime in the 14th century B.C. and vanishing only a few years later. He is typically identified as a high priest or a wielder of magic. Those less charitably inclined in the modern age see him as a charlatan who fooled his followers. Many Egyptologists believe he never even existed, as there is little contemporary evidence.

According to legend, there were dozens of the Kenk priestesses, all of whom committed suicide when Kentenkamen vanished …

The more interesting part of the legend to this author is the modern myth of the cult. To many native Egyptians, the Kenk priestesses have obtained a reputation as an Egyptian "Cassandra," warning of danger to come. Stories persist of the priestesses appearing to people throughout the world warning of dire consequences. Legend among the modern followers has it that the priestesses have warned people of coming personal troubles, as well as several major events, including the burial of Pompei in 79 A.D., the 1754 Cairo Earthquake, the 1816 "Year Without a Summer," and the 1914 assassination of Archduke Franz Ferdinand of Austria. These claims have always come to light after the event, offering no proof of their veracity.

September 28, 1922
Entry in Journal of Blake Randolph

Breakfast with both Douglas and Bradley in my cabin. They are convinced I was warned by a member of this cult, or at least someone who thinks they are a member of the Kenk.

"The best-case scenario is that she is off her rocker, but harmless," Douglas speculated. "But she could also be disturbed and quite dangerous. Or worse she's a member of this cult."

"You can't possibly believe that!" I responded, shocked that he would even entertain the idea. "This is the 1920s! The time of myths is over."

"Blake, you've spent your entire life in the Western world, mostly in America. In the grand scheme of things, we are but babies. These societies go back beyond history. The people and tribes I've seen have erased any doubts I may have had about the spiritual world. There are things we cannot understand."

"Gentleman, if I may," Bradley interrupted. "I believe the most likely conclusion is that she is a member of this cult or some similar group, but it is nothing to worry about. There are many groups in my adopted home that object to what they see as the 'pillaging' of their national treasures. She found out about the reason for your visit to Egypt and decided to make some ill-advised attempt to frighten you off.

"Perhaps she even found out that Dr. Prowse is looking for this Kentenkamen fellow. You have no idea about the expedition?"

Shaking my head, I replied, "No, Dr. Prowse has been very closed-mouthed. I suppose it could be."

"Well, there you go. As for why we haven't seen her since then," he said, raising a finger in anticipation of Douglas's question. "That's fairly simple. It's unlikely a woman would be traveling alone. She is likely on the ship with her husband, brother, father, a chaperone of some sort. They have heard of her action and, seeking to avoid embarrassment for her hysterical female behavior, have made sure she doesn't leave her cabin. Quite simple, when you think about it."

I had to admit that made sense, but Douglas was less accepting of the argument.

"I believe this situation is more dangerous than either of you recognize, but I see I'm not going to convince you.

"Well, I am at a bit of loose ends right now, so perhaps I should see if there's any more room on this expedition of yours. If you're too stubborn to protect yourself, then somebody needs to watch your back."

"I'd welcome your companionship, Douglas, but I'm merely along for the ride here. This is Dr. Prowse's expedition."

"At the very least, I can meet the good doctor and warn him of this. I'm sure I can convince him to let me join the party."

"Top-notch idea! I'd love to meet the great man myself," Bradley chimed in. "So it's decided – when we arrive in Alexandria, we'll all meet the famous Dr. Prowse!"

"He doesn't by any chance have a daughter, does he?" Douglas asked with a smile. "The Egyptologist always has a beautiful daughter in the pulps."

"No, thanks be to God, he doesn't," I responded, shaking my head.

Douglas may be a different man than the one I fought with in France, but it's good to know that some things don't change.

Our triumvirate parted ways for most of the day. I took advantage of Bradley's library to do some more reading on the history of Egypt. The man is still annoying, but has ended up being more useful than I first suspected.

We arrive in Alexandria tomorrow.

Egypt News & Mail
September 28, 1922
Dr. Prowse Returns for New Expedition

Dr. James Prowse, one of the leading experts on ancient Egypt, has returned from his sabbatical in London to mount a new expedition.

While Dr. Prowse has been characteristically secretive about the details of his search, he did grant an exclusive interview with our correspondent. The renowned Egyptologist is in Alexandria this week preparing his team for their foray into the desert.

"We are quite confident that we are on the verge of a great discovery," Prowse told the News & Mail. "The initial research and digging we have done indicates an undiscovered tomb of great importance. I think we will be rewriting the history books when we are done."

Dr. Prowse did offer that he will not be searching for the tomb of King Tutenkhamen, noting that he believes his former colleague Howard Carter is close to unearthing the final resting place of the boy king.

"As far as we know, what we have discovered is a heretofore unknown burial site, and we look forward to announcing our find shortly," Prowse said.

While unwilling to offer a certain date for his announcement, Prowse said he expects to be able to share his discovery in the near future ...

September 29, 1922
Entry in Journal of Blake Randolph

(Evening)

It has been an eventful day and no opportunity to write before now. We arrived in Alexandria today and are now safely ensconced in the Crown Hotel.

The ship docked here midday. Douglas and I agreed to split up to watch the departures for the mysterious woman who visited me enroute. No luck. Douglas believed this bolstered his claim; I was more inclined to believe she departed at another time or port.

A driver was waiting at the port to take us to Dr. Prowse's temporary office at the Alexandria Museum. As agreed, Douglas and Bradley joined me to meet the doctor. That was to be the last time anything went according to plan.

Dr. Prowse sighed as we entered his office in the bowels of the museum.

"It appears I was right to send a driver," he said. "I feared you had not received my wire when there was no response."

"Wire?" I responded, confused at that point.

"Yes, Blake, I'm afraid the expedition is in danger. I had attempted to send you a telegram before you left New York, but it appears I missed you."

"But doctor," Douglas interrupted, holding up a copy of the local paper he had picked up when we arrived in the city. "This article makes it seem like the expedition is days away from success."

Dr. Prowse seemed to notice my companions for the first time, taking in the motley crew with a glance.

"I'm afraid you have me at a disadvantage, Mr. …?"

I quickly apologized and made introductions.

"Yes, yes, good to meet you. The article … well, let us consider that a little effort at publicity. I have investors that would be quite unhappy to find our efforts on the verge of collapse."

"If money's the issue …" I started.

"No, Blake, it's not money. It's people. These damn superstitious fools! We had a team of 12 men on the initial dig. After we returned to Alexandria, one of our guides was trampled by a camel, of all things. He died. One of the others ended up in the hospital with some sort of stomach ailment. That was all it took to convince them the dig was cursed.

"I've sent a local driver and a guide back to secure the site. Besides my nephew Charles, the rest of the team is made up of local men. Those five have refused to go back. They've spread the word with the locals, so there's no help to be found there."

I asked Dr. Prowse how many we needed to manage the dig.

"The five of us aren't enough, not to mention we need another guide if we're going to try to safely manage this."

"How about six?" Douglas offered.

"Or seven? It could be quite an adventure," Bradley chimed in. "All I have to do is send a wire to my business partner, let him know the change in plans."

"I appreciate the enthusiasm, gentlemen, but it's no easy task, especially if you're unfamiliar with the land."

Douglas quickly jumped in to detail his background as not only a soldier, but also his adventures since the war ended.

"And I have been in Egypt for more than a decade and studying it even longer," Bradley offered. "I dare say, you won't find many men who know more about its people and history."

Bradley, unsurprisingly, continued to pontificate for several minutes, demonstrating his knowledge … and inability to know when to stop talking.

The problem, the doctor offered at that point, was that we still required a guide.

"I may know just the man for the job," Bradley said. "A rather horrible man, only cares about money, but won't be scared off by any curse. If I can find him, he'll do it, I wager."

Dr. Prowse, it seemed, was convinced. "It just might work. Eight men ... if we all pitch in. Yes, that could do it."

"Now that we're all on the team, tell us, Doctor – are we hunting for Kentenkamen?" Douglas asked.

That shocked the good doctor, who seemed at a loss for words for a few moments.

"Bloody hell!" he finally responded. "How in the world did you know that?"

I recounted my encounter on the ship, as well as all that happened afterward. Bradley and Douglas jumped in with their thoughts and insights. After his initial shock, the doctor seemed to take the news in stride, noting it was just one more obstacle. He seemed inclined to believe there was a simple explanation – that one of the crew working on the dig had stumbled onto their goal and shared the information.

While only Prowse, his nephew and his assistant knew the true goal of the expedition, he admitted that it would not have been difficult for someone else to figure it out.

"But let's keep this information to ourselves, gentlemen. We don't need to scare anyone else off."

He stood again, signaling it was time to leave. "There's work to do if we're going to be ready to depart tomorrow. Prepare yourselves men. And find us that guide, Mr. Bradley."

Bradley insisted on visiting his potential guide on his own, so Douglas and I made for the hotel. Only a few minutes ago he arrived at our room to let us know his effort was successful.

Tomorrow morning we head to the desert!

OPPORTUNITY TO JOIN EXPEDITION. RETURN TO CAIRO
DELAYED. HAVE HIRED GAMAL.

We are somewhere in the desert outside Alexandria, enroute
to the dig. According to Dr. Prowse it is a roughly eight-hour
drive. We are making the trip in a British Army lorry left behind
after the war. They are not designed for comfort!

Gamal, Bradley's guide, is driving. I have attempted to
engage him in conversation a few times, but he seems to have
little interest.

"He's not a friendly man, but as long as we pay him, he'll get
the job done," Bradley had confided in us before we departed. I
suppose beggars can't be choosers.

As it turns out, most of our supplies are British Army surplus.
Charles, the doctor's nephew, was one of the army's combat
cameramen during the war, and still has many connections there.
He's a surprisingly soft-spoken man, not what you would expect
from that crew. Those men who operated the Aeroscopes during
the war to capture the battlefield footage were a brave, often
reckless, lot. The Aeroscope was called the "camera of death" for
a good reason.

Before we left this morning, Dr. Prowse told us why Charles
has joined us for this expedition. He will be operating a new type
of movie camera that has sound! I had heard such things were
being worked on, but this is the first time I have actually seen
one.

Charles became quite animated when discussing the new
technology.

"This device arrived just two days ago. It is called a

'Fowlercam.' It's quite an ingenious little machine, developed by a fellow named Fowler – based on the work of the American Lee de Forest, I understand."

The camera, like the Aeroscope, seemed to have been designed with mobility in mind.

"This Fowler made an attempt to sell it to some of the movie studios in England and failed quite spectacularly. There were also rumors of a lawsuit. He fled London ahead of the creditors and lawyers, but left this behind. It ended up in the hands of a mate of mine from university, along with plenty of film."

Dr. Prowse smiled. "Charles is quite enthralled with the technology. I admit I don't understand a bit of it, but the publicity we could get from films of our expedition could be quite beneficial."

I've asked Charles to show me how to use the camera. The whole thing is quite fascinating.

That's enough for now. The ride is quite bumpy.

Fowlercam transcript
September 30, 1922

This is the first of several transcripts from what I can only assume was film shot during the expedition. I can find no film in any of my uncle's records. Based on what I have read here about the success of those efforts to film, it's no surprise the Fowlercam has faded into history. – DR

"Film degraded/sound spotty" (hand-written note at top of transcript)

Dr. Prowse: Greetings! We have embarked on our journey to the tomb of Kentenkamen. We have stopped along the way and soon […] so I will keep this brief.

Our goal is that this will be the most documented […] undertaken in this country. The goal of science is to enlighten and we hope you will find our documentation of this journey to be educational and exciting!

Voice offscreen: We must continue if we are to keep our schedule, doctor!

Dr. Prowse: There you have it! Our adventure continues!

September 30, 1922
Entry in Journal of Blake Randolph

(Evening)
We finally arrived at the site. The ride was closer to ten hours than eight. It is nearly dark, so little to be done tonight. We met the rest of the team: the guide Neil McCoy and the driver and cook Youssef. The Egyptian seemed nervous, but was much friendlier than Gamal. I was surprised to find that the guide was named "McCoy," having been expecting an Egyptian. Instead, he was a thin, Scottish man of indeterminate age.

Dr. Prowse tells us he has lived in the desert outside Alexandria for decades. He is considered a bit of an eccentric, but knows the area better than almost any native. He has been searching for Kentenkamen for even longer than the doctor.

They report the site is secured and Dr. Prowse expects us to be able to make significant progress tomorrow.

Fowlercam transcript
October 1, 1922

[Prowse is standing in front of an excavated site]

Dr. Prowse: Good morning. I am Dr. James Prowse. It is October 1, 1922, approximately 8 a.m. local time. Behind me you see what we believe is the entrance to the tomb of Kentenkamen. Virtually unknown today, he was an influential figure in the 14th Century B.C. He had a reputation as a wizard, a prophet, a ... well, he was seen as a supernatural figure, in fact. We on this expedition certainly put no stock in that, but there is a small group of followers who still believe in him today. More importantly, we want to uncover more about this mysterious man, who is said to have been an adviser to Amenhotep III and Akhenaten, but has almost completely disappeared from the historic record.

We know we have uncovered a structure of some sort and our research indicates this is the final resting place of the prophet. Unlike other important figures in ancient Egypt, he has been entombed in this remote place. It has taken me more than 20 years to find this site.
(turning to look off camera) Does it make sense to go into the research now?
[inaudible answer]

Dr. Prowse: I have extensively documented my work over the last two decades in my journals that reside at the British Museum, so let's not get bogged down in details. The most interesting part of the quest to most of you, I assume, would be what brought us here. The final piece of information, interestingly enough, was uncovered in records captured by British troops from the Ottoman Empire during the recent war.
But back to today's work. Let's move this way now, Charles.
[Camera angle changes as Dr. Prowse moves closer to site.]
You can see what appears to be a shape that could be an entrance or doorway here. Our belief is that beyond this lies that which we have been seeking. I have to admit that being this close after all these years is quite exciting.

That's enough for now, Charles, let's ...

(midday)

Success!

We have cleared the opening and will be entering the tomb soon. Dr. Prowse insists we take a lunch break as we have been working for seven hours and he wants no mistakes.

Dr. Prowse has explained more about Kentenkamen than he wished to share for the film he is making. All the official histories of the era make no mention of the man. It is as if he has been wiped from history. All that remains are rumors, myths, supernatural explanations. The strangest part of all of this is that he has been buried out here in the middle of nowhere. According to what Dr. Prowse has been able to uncover, it was this Kenk cult that built this shrine to him, spiriting his body away from an unmarked grave. But this is all based on stories about stories about stories, written centuries later.

My visitor on the ship shows that there are still at least some here aware of this history …

[Dr. Prowse is standing in front of the entrance.]

Dr. Prowse: As you can see, our entrance is now open. We are about to step inside. That means those of you watching this are seeing it just as we saw it.

Our guide, Neil McCoy, has checked the footing inside to make sure it is safe, but other than that we have not inspected the site. As you can see, we are all equipped with lights. I will be the first to step in, followed by our cameraman Charles.

[Prowse steps in, camera moves to follow. Picture fades to black at this

point. Crew appears to be unaware that it is too dark to capture images.]

Dr. Prowse: We are in what appears to be an entrance chamber of some sort. There is a tunnel on the opposite side of the room … we'll explore that soon. Charles, bring the camera over here. You can see here above the entrance an engraving of some sort … we need more light. Blake? Perfect. It is partially damaged, but … it says " … restful slumber … the great Kentenkamen … " Yes, it is him! Let me go on … more is obscured, but then it says " … only believers may enter and be found worthy. To all others death will come."

[unidentified voice]: That's certainly comforting.

Dr. Prowse: I think it's important for our audience to know that these types of warnings are quite common. The idea that there can be a curse is ridiculous. Warnings like these were put in place to warn grave robbers away, to try to protect the belongings of the dead. The Egyptians are a superstitious people and are very likely to be scared off by this sort of warning.

Now, let's look around the rest of this room. Over here we see paintings depicting a jackal, most likely Anubis, the god of mummification and the afterlife. There is quite a bit of imagery reflecting him in fact. You can see two jackal-headed soldiers flanking each side of the tunnel as well. Quite sinister-looking chaps, actually.

As we would expect, there is little in the way of artifacts or treasure in this opening chamber. We are literally surrounded by depictions of death for those that dare to enter the tomb. It appears the goal here was to ensure any would-be grave robbers were dissuaded from moving beyond this antechamber.

Speaking of caution, I am noticing a very strong odor in here. That is all too common when entering a space like this that has not been opened for centuries. In the spirit of safety, and recognition that it will soon be dark, I believe we will step outside and wait until tomorrow to explore further.

October 1, 1922
Entry in Journal of Blake Randolph

We've just finished at the site. Youssef is preparing food, but I wanted to get some thoughts down before supper.

Some of the paintings in there were … quite violent. I can see how they would scare away someone who tended to be superstitious. I believe they have only heightened the uneasiness Douglas feels about this trip. Bradley and Gamal did not enter the chamber with us, and seem unconcerned, as do McCoy and Dr. Prowse. Youssef is even more nervous than they were when we arrived.

I am excited about what we will discover tomorrow when we can finally enter. I understand the doctor's caution and must defer to his expertise, but the wait will be difficult. I don't imagine I will be able to sleep much tonight!

(later)
Supper is over, but that's not the important event tonight.

I stepped outside after that last entry, only to see that Gamal was arguing with Youssef in Arabic, with Gamal gesturing as he yelled at his fellow Egyptian. Youssef shoved Gamal, prompting the guide to launch himself at the cook, wrapping his hands around Youssef's neck.

"Hey!" I shouted and began running toward the men. Bradley and Douglas, coming from the other direction, arrived at the melee before I did. By this time, the two men were on the ground, rolling dangerously close to the fire.

"Gentlemen … " Bradley started, reaching out to the two and getting a punch in the stomach in response from a flailing arm. As he fell to the ground, Douglas and I charged in, me grabbing Gamal and Douglas Youssef.

"Let go of me, Yankee," Gamal spat at me, wrestling away from me.

"Gamal, what was that about?"

He threw up his hands in obvious disgust. "He is a superstitious fool, bah!" he said, gesturing back toward Youssef. "He is scared of this Kent-man you have found. Wanted me to help him get away from here. He's a coward!"

"Yes, there is evil here, but he is a liar!" Youssef shouted back, looking at Dr. Prowse, who, along with McCoy and Charles, had now arrived at the disturbance.

"Doctor, he is a … a … a … criminal. A bad man! I know him. He try to steal from us!"

"He's just trying to cover up his cowardice. Men like him are why all of you look down on us. Bah – my job was to get you here, not to put up with the rest of this," Gamal finished before storming away toward the vehicles.

Bradley had now caught his breath and regained his footing and injected himself in the conversation.

"I suppose much of this is on me, gentlemen. I told you Gamal was a man of rather low character. His loyalty can be bought, though. I have worked with him before. I will talk to him. In his own way, he can be managed."

With that, Bradley followed after the guide leaving the rest of us around the fire.

Dr. Prowse quickly ascertained that Youssef was not injured. In his broken English, Youssef assured us that while he believed there was danger here, he would not leave the team.

"Youssef is a loyal man," McCoy offered. "He has been a great help throughout the dig. He can be trusted. Now this Gamal fellow, on the other hand, strikes me as one we cannot trust."

There was general agreement on that point.

(later)

It is shortly after 9 p.m. I'm not sure where to start. With the facts, I suppose.

About an hour ago, I woke to a commotion outside my tent. I rushed out to find Dr. Prowse, Douglas and Charles gathered around McCoy, who was laying on the ground, staring up, dead-eyed, with a look of terror frozen on his face.

"What happened?" I asked of no one in particular.

"That is what we are trying to ascertain, Blake," Prowse responded. "It appears McCoy has ... well, you can see for yourself."

"He looks like he was scared to death," Douglas said. "I found him like this when I came out to fill my canteen. I haven't seen a man look like that since the war."

"I told you there was evil here!"

We all turned to look at Youssef, who had appeared behind us. In the fading light of the campfire, I could also see Bradley and Gamal approaching.

"We must leave this place now!" Youssef continued. "The curse of Kentenkamen cannot be ignored."

Dr. Prowse sighed, running his hand over his face.

"There is no curse, Youssef!" Prowse paused, gathering himself. "I apologize, but this curse is nothing but superstitious nonsense. McCoy was not a healthy man. He had a heart condition, but insisted on being here for the discovery.

"As for leaving, we certainly need to get McCoy's body back to civilization so he can have a proper burial, but we can't leave in the middle of the night. Driving across the desert in the dark is a good way to get ourselves killed.

"We will leave in the morning. That is the sanest thing to do. Let's move McCoy inside the tomb. It is cooler there and the body will be safer. As for the watch, we're going to double up so nobody is out here alone. Youssef, you'll join Mr. Morrow. In three hours, Mr. Bradley and Mr. Randolph will take over. Charles and I will do duties after that. When first light comes we will prepare to leave."

It is now almost 11 p.m. and still sleep escapes me.

I have gone from great excitement over our find to great disappointment. I suppose that sounds horrible, but I'll admit there is a part of me that wants to stay here and explore the tomb rather than have to haul McCoy back to Alexandria.

(later)

Almost midnight and little sleep. Must have dozed off a little. Thought I heard something outside, but probably my imagination. At this point, I might as well join Douglas and Youssef early.

October 2, 1922
Entry in Journal of Blake Randolph

That idiot!

Youssef was obviously more scared than we thought. He has fled with one of the trucks!

Unable to sleep, I stepped out earlier than expected and found Douglas unconscious on the ground near the fire, a good-sized lump on the back of his head. I was able to bring him around by splashing some water in his face, but he wasn't sure exactly what happened.

"It was more than an hour after everyone else went to sleep," he said. "Youssef was still nervous, jumping at every sound. He said he was thirsty, was going to get some water. Asked me if I wanted any, but I said no. Have my canteen here.

"A minute or two later, I heard something behind me, started to turn, and then ... that's all I remember. He gave me a good wallop, that I can tell you," he said, gingerly touching the back of his head.

It was at that point that we awakened the rest of the team. A search of the camp found no sign of Youssef … and the absence of one of the trucks.

"I told you he was a superstitious coward," Gamal stated smugly as we gathered around the fire. "Now look at the mess you've gotten yourself into."

"That's enough, Gamal," Bradley snapped. "I vouched for you with these people. If you're not going to be helpful, just shut up."

"You're all fools. Let me know when you're ready to leave. It can't be soon enough for me."

"Gamal, we should all stay together – " Dr. Prowse started as the guide began to leave.

"I am safer away from all of you!" Gamal shouted as he continued walking away.

Dr. Prowse looked at the rest of us, shaking his head.

"Unfortunately, with only one truck, we cannot even come close to getting all of our people and equipment back to Alexandria. We will all squeeze into our last truck at first light and try to return with more trucks. I fear that we will not be able to get any local help once people hear of this!

"Now, I have a proposal. We have almost six hours until sunrise. Speaking for myself, I don't imagine I will be able to sleep. Not knowing when we will be able to return, I propose we explore the tomb now."

Charles was the first to speak up.

"Uncle, I'm not sure. So much has happened already …"

"There is nothing to fear besides bad luck. A man with a heart condition had a heart attack and a superstitious man panicked. This is our chance! Who knows what will happen once we get back to Alexandria? There will be more questions, investigations, someone else could get back here ahead of us."

Bradley looked around our little band and shrugged his

shoulders.

"In all fairness, we have little to do before we leave. It would be a productive use of our time."

Eager to see what lay in the tomb, I readily agreed. Douglas, while less enthusiastic, conceded the point.

Fowlercam transcript
October 2, 1922

[Picture dark, shadows and shades of gray]

Dr. Prowse: We have passed through the doorway that was guarded by those two jackal-soldiers and down the short tunnel. We now find ourselves in a chamber that measures approximately 10,000 square feet. As you can see, the treasure here is greater than we imagined.

Gold, jewels … it is really quite amazing. As in the outer chamber, the room is decorated with imagery of jackals. Look over here and you will see that in every corner of the room we find these jackal statues, measuring nearly eight feet tall, reaching from the floor to the ceiling.

Now, over here, we have a small table, quite interesting. There are six large blue stones, quite possibly sapphires, arranged in a pattern around these hieroglyphics. A piece of the wall seems to have fallen on the table as well. *Blake take this, please. Here you go.* As I was saying, these stones seem to point out the importance of this message. I'm not familiar with some of the symbols here, but definitely recognize "eye" and "Kentenkamen." This will bear more study.

Unfortunately, it appears there is no tomb of Kentenkamen here. This room is packed with treasure and everyday belongings, as we would expect to ease his transit to the afterlife. My hope is that means there is a hidden room of some sort where we will find the actual resting place.

It is quite common for there to be multiple chambers before we get to the final resting place. During my work on the tomb of Pahotep, we found a similar situation where a loose stone allowed us to discover a system of weights and counterweights that opened an unknown chamber.

There is a thin layer of dusty sand on the floor, but otherwise, we have to imagine this room looks like it did when the tomb was built.

You will also notice the large collection of furniture and other materials. We have found chairs, tables, even dishware. These would be the items buried with the Kentenkamen for his use in the afterlife.

What time is it?

Charles [behind camera]: Almost 3 a.m.

Let's pause here, Charles. Shut that off.

Fowlercam transcript
October 2, 1922

[Picture dark]

Dr. Prowse: Greetings again. Our search thus far has revealed no hidden entries. It is nearly sunrise here, not that one can tell inside the tomb.

For reasons beyond our control, we will need to soon stop our search for now. We fully intend to continue our search at another date. But before we do that, I do want to show our audience one interesting item we did uncover.

This wall contains some interesting imagery, showing a large group of women worshipping what appears to be a man bathed in light. As you may remember from our earlier discussion, the followers of Kentenkamen were said to be entirely female. Now, there is also an interesting message here.

If you step this way and get a better view of this ...

Charles look out!

[Crashing sound; what little of picture is visible blurs in a flash of motion]

[Jumble of overlapping voices, mostly inaudible]
The statue ... on top of him
Move it carefully ... is he ...
What about ... careful!
Dead ... crushed his skull ...

The transcript indicates that the camera continued to record at this point, but the conversation is difficult to follow and much of it was not picked up by the damaged camera. We do have a typed account, apparently written at a later date by Blake Randolph. – DR

Typed account of Blake Randolph (undated)

One of the large jackal statues had fallen, crushing Charles. There was no doubt the injury was mortal. A silence had descended over our entire band.

We had obviously pushed our luck as far as we could. As a foolish young man, I had not believed in the supernatural. At that moment, I was convinced I had been wrong. As it turned out, I was both right and wrong.

"I'm afraid he's dead, sir," Douglas said after examining Charles.

Dr. Prowse sank down slowly, sitting on a stone bench. In just two minutes he had seemingly aged a decade.

"I know, Douglas," he said. "I know. All my fault ... how will I tell my sister I've killed her only son?"

I attempted to comfort the doctor, but could offer little solace.

"It's not your fault, doctor. He bumped into the statue, it was unstable. It was an accident."

"No," he said, shaking his head. "It's my fault he was here, my fault I insisted on exploring instead of waiting. My fault for ignoring the warnings.

"Maybe we really are cursed," he added, his voice breaking.

I was about to respond when we were interrupted by a laugh from the dark entrance.

"Now you believe in curses, I see? That is very funny. Let me assure you, there is no curse here. Just stupid interlopers," Gamal said as he stepped into the light.

"For the love of God, Gamal," I shouted. "Now is hardly the time!"

By the time the words were out, I had registered the revolver in his hand.

The guide smiled, gesturing with the gun at the fallen statue. "For what it's worth, that was meant for you, doctor. Although it really doesn't matter. None of you are leaving this chamber."

"What are you talking about?" Douglas said. "Are you one of those fanatics who want to keep foreigners out of the country?"

Gamal grimaced at that. "Oh, please no. I'm no superstitious fool like that idiot Youssef. Oh, he and the truck are about a mile out that way, by the way, past that large dune," he said, gesturing to the west.

"You killed him?" Bradley asked. "McCoy, too?"

Gamal glanced at Bradley, a slightly perplexed look on his face.

"Of course. McCoy was a simple matter of an Egyptian Cobra left under his hat by the fire.

"But in answer to your question, I'm just in it for the money. These treasures belong to me. I was promised them for, let's say, services rendered.

"No, no, I intend to sell these to the highest bidder. History is just that, history. Who cares about these dusty artifacts?"

Gamal paused, looking at each of us.

"Now, as I was saying, the statue was quite simple to rig to fall. I honestly had expected that the doctor would examine the engraving at the base and trip the cord I placed there. It seems your inept nephew stumbled upon it first."

At that, the previously listless doctor lunged at Gamal. "Why you worthless –"

The rest of the sentence was cut off by the report of Gamal's Enfield. The bullet hit the doctor in his chest, stopping him in his tracks.

"Now, I hope we won't have any other interruptions."

I rushed to the doctor's side. He was unconscious; still alive, but bleeding badly. With medical attention hours away, I knew we couldn't save him.

"You bastard! He's going to die!"

"Really not my problem. The only thing I have to decide now is what order I kill you in. It is freeing not to have to make them look like accidents anymore. All my employer has asked is that I kill you, but I think we can have some fun first."

"You're a bloody madman," Douglas said.

"I enjoy killing people, yes, but I'm quite sane. And quite good at it. The British army trained me when you brought your stupid war to our country and it turned out I liked it quite a bit. As it turns out, the money is a lot better when you're not working for an occupying force."

Gamal laughed again, continuing to wave the pistol about.

I glanced at Douglas, who nodded ever so slightly. We knew we had to take out this madman, but before we could make any move, another shot rang out. Realizing I was unhurt, I looked quickly at Douglas, fearing the worst.

It was then that I realized the report had come from the smoking Luger in Bradley's hand. Gamal toppled to the floor, dead from the head shot.

"Well, that was getting quite annoying," Bradley offered. "The man was giving me a headache."

Douglas and I both looked at Bradley, who no longer appeared the inept academic, in shock. Douglas was the first to break the silence. "Well done, Bradley!" he said, stepping toward him. "How did you …"

Bradley turned the Luger in our direction. "Quite far enough, both of you. You're going to stay right there."

He walked backwards, putting more space between us and him.

I cursed myself for not having figured it out earlier. It had all been an act, obviously. Bradley had wormed his way into our expedition, coming up with answers and solutions when we needed them. He had told us about Kentenkamen, he had sought me out on the ship, he had brought Gamal to us. Every step of the way, he had made sure the expedition continued.

"This can't just be about the treasure," I said.

Bradley smiled, agreeing.

"For Gamal it was. He was a tool. A tool that had outlived its usefulness.

"I'm afraid you have stumbled into something much bigger than you ever imagined. You've both proven yourselves to be brave men – we can use more soldiers and the rewards are quite plentiful."

Douglas, exasperated, asked what he was talking about.

"I suppose I owe you that much. Let's start with this: it's all true. Kentenkamen was real, he was powerful and his power continues today. The cult of Kenk, the prophecies. You cannot imagine the effect he has had on the world. And it needs to stop."

One of us must have reacted silently, because he laughed.

"That's not what you were expecting, I see. I'll make it quite simple: I am part of an organization, one that has been around for centuries. No, we don't have a silly name like these Egyptians. We have certain plans, and Kentenkamen continues to interfere with them. There are weak people throughout the world and they need to be eliminated, controlled. We have made great strides in that direction, but with Kentenkamen and his disciples out of the way, our ability to improve this world will be unchecked.

"Oh, don't look so shocked. You're Americans. How is this any different than your colonial efforts in Cuba or the Philippines? Or what you have done to the natives of your country? You had to fight a war to figure out slavery was wrong!"

"America is a force for good!" Douglas shouted. "We may not always get it right, but –"

Bradley waved the gun in his direction, silencing him.

"You stumble around like the children you are. But that's neither here nor there. Today, you have a chance to help me right this ship we call Earth."

I found my voice. "Why would we help you?"

"Because it is your only chance to survive. You have a choice: assist me with my search, or I kill you now and conduct my own efforts. It will take me longer without your help, but a few hours is nothing in a quest that has lasted centuries."

We saw little choice. Helping him now would give us more time to figure out a way out of this mess.

"Fine," Douglas said. I nodded my assent as well.

"Good. That was the answer I was hoping for. As I said, I do really believe the two of you would come around to our side if you thought about it. The world is dangerous, full of chaos. You both fought in the war; you've seen what that chaos brings us."

"You've made your point, Bradley," I said through clenched teeth. "Get on with it."

He nodded, accepting my statement.

"There is another chamber beyond this one. That is where Kentenkamen reposes. It is not, as the doctor assumed, a tomb. For Kentenkamen is not dead, merely in a period of stasis. That is why his power continues.

"Our goal is quite simple: find the chamber, open the sarcophagus and kill him with this," Bradley said, removing a 12-inch blade, made entirely of a black glass-like substance, from his satchel. "He is immune to earthly efforts, but this … this is quite special."

I gestured around the room.

"In case you forgot, Bradley, we've been looking for that chamber for hours."

He nodded again. "True, but I'm afraid I had some information I had kept to myself. There is a settlement near Alexandria that housed disciples of Kentenkamen until last week. Thanks to some associates in the Egyptian army we made short work of those protectors.

"They were quite loyal and fought to the death, but really had little chance against our modern technology. We managed to keep one of them alive and a little creative interrogation revealed a significant clue. All we needed then was the information we had sought for centuries: where was his so-called 'tomb.' Thanks to the good doctor, I finally have that answer."

He removed a piece of paper from his satchel and slowly set it on a nearby chair, then backed away, keeping his eyes and pistol on us the entire time.

"That is what you are looking for. It should be somewhere near the east wall. I'm going to stay right here where I can watch you."

I picked up the paper, shining my light on it as Douglas looked over my shoulder. It had a sketch that roughly resembled a rising sun.

"I don't think we have a choice," Douglas whispered. "We have to bide our time." I nodded slightly, and we both moved toward the east wall.

Clearing the sand away along that side, we quickly uncovered the symbol. It was about a yard from the wall, roughly halfway between the north and south walls. Seeing that, Bradley rolled a flashlight to Douglas.

"Stand on the sun," Bradley said. "Point the torch at that jewel over his heart," indicating a glossy stone on the chest of the jackal in the southwest corner of the chamber.

Douglas turned on the flashlight, which had a cover of some sort that blocked most of the light. It emitted a small beam of red light that danced around the jackal's torso before coming to rest on the stone. The heart seemed to glow on its own now, reflecting the light back to the east wall in an even brighter beam. The beam landed on one of the paintings that decorated that side of the room, on the head of an asp, some five feet above the ground.

"Randolph, push on that spot!"

I rushed over, excited in spite of myself. I pushed lightly, with no luck. I increased my pressure, but still found nothing but unmoving stone. Finally, stepping back, I leaned into the wall, putting both hands on the asp, with my full weight behind me.

All at once, a stone about a foot square gave way, sliding back at least 12 inches. At the same time. I heard a rumbling sound from the south wall opposite the tunnel through which we had entered. The seemingly solid wall slid to the side, revealing a 6-foot-tall doorway. Douglas and I both moved toward the new opening.

"Yes! Yes! Finally!" Bradley shouted, dancing from foot to foot with glee. "Our moment of triumph –"

Before he could finish his sentence, a similar rumbling sound came from the tunnel to the north. We all turned in that direction, only to see a large slab of stone slam down, blocking the exit.

"Ahh!" Bradley shouted, now in anger.

Both Douglas and I took advantage of Bradley's distraction to move in front of the new opening.

"No! No! No!" Bradley continued to rage at the blocked door, pounding at it with his left fist while keeping his grip on the Luger in his right.

Douglas chuckled briefly.

"I think maybe that fellow you tortured left something out of his explanation," he said with a smile. "I had a feeling I wasn't going to get out of here alive, but I'm glad you're not going to either."

That prompted Bradley to turn back toward us, Luger still firmly in hand.

"SHUT UP!" he shouted at us, with a mad look in his eyes, before gathering himself.

He continued in an eerily calm voice: "I might die, but not before I kill him. I haven't come this far to let Kentenkamen live. But I don't need either of you for that."

Bradley opened fire. Douglas crashed into me and, then, blackness.

[No picture/audio only]

Douglas Morrow: I think maybe that fellow you tortured left something out of his explanation. I had a feeling I wasn't going to get out of here alive, but I'm glad you're not going to either.

Quincey Bradley: Shut up! *[shouted]* I might die, but not before I kill him. I haven't come this far to let Kentenkamen live. But I don't need either of you for that.

[shots fired; at least four]
[large crashing sound]

Bradley: No! No! Open up, damn it! *[pounding sound]*
[two additional shots fired]

Bradley: This isn't over!
[unidentifiable sound – scraping of stone?]
Bradley: What the – ? Oh, God, no, no, stay away
[one shot, then clicking of empty chamber]
Bradley: No, no – ahhhhh!!! *[screams]*

Entry in Journal of Blake Randolph, written by Douglas Morrow
Undated (written October 2, 1922)

Blake – I found this journal and pencil in your pocket. Hope you don't mind that I appropriated this page, but I'm a little worried that I'm not going to be alive by the time you wake up.

One of Bradley's shots got me in the stomach. We both know what that means. Maybe you'll be able to get out of here alive, so I wanted you to know what happened.

After Bradley started shooting at us, we both jumped for the door to this chamber. As we crashed through the door, I felt the shot hit me. You must have hit the floor or wall, as you've got a good-sized lump on your head.

As soon as we were through the doorway, the stone slid back across it, sealing us in here in the dark. I still had my flashlight, so I can see well enough to write this note. This would seem to be the burial chamber for which Prowse and Bradley were looking.

Bradley started yelling and pounding at the door, but it didn't move. That was quickly followed by what I can only describe as screams of terror. I can only assume that something or someone attacked Bradley. I thought I heard movement beyond the wall, but it is now silent again.

You have been a good friend, Blake. I am honored to have served at your side one final time.

Your friend,
Douglas

Typed account of Blake Randolph (undated)

I slowly awoke, as if coming out of a fog. As I started to move, I fought off a wave of dizziness. Someone shined a flashlight in my face.

"It's about time," Douglas said, wincing as he leaned over me.

He was leaning against a stone container of some sort. I dragged myself over next to him. With the limited light I could see we were in another large chamber, but most of the room was in darkness.

"Are you hurt?" I asked.

"You could say that," he said, groaning as he lifted his shirt to show me the wound in his torso.

"Oh, damn it, Douglas. I'm sorry I dragged you into this. There's got to be –"

"Sit down," he said as I started to rise. "We're not going

anywhere. The door slammed shut as soon as we got in. That's probably the only thing that kept Bradley from finishing us off."

I stood up again. "We're not done yet, Douglas. Maybe I can talk Bradley into letting us out. We can take the truck and I can get you to a doctor. We can still …"

"I've looked and it's solid stone," he replied. "If there's a way out, I can't find it.

"There's no way I'm surviving a trip across that desert out there, either. And based on the screaming I heard while you were knocked out, Bradley is no longer in any position to help anybody."

"That's certainly true," a voice responded from the darkness.

We both spun in that direction, Morrow giving out a small grunt as he did so.

From the rear of the chamber, a small light began to shine, growing to light the entire room as bright as a sunlit day. The light seemed to originate from a golden sarcophagus against the far wall. I immediately recognized the woman standing in front of it.

"Is that … ?" Douglas trailed off.

"Yes, that's her."

"Blake Randolph," she began. "We are pleased to see you have survived. Our vision of the future was cloudy and we were uncertain of your fate. The master will also be pleased."

"The master?" Douglas asked. "Kentenkamen?"

"Ahh, Douglas Morrow. I have a feeling it was your presence here that ensured the survival of Blake Randolph. We were unable to foresee the presence of the one who calls himself Bradley, but it seems that we also underestimated you," she said with a smile.

"But in answer to your question, yes, I refer to Kentenkamen."

Douglas gasped in pain, reminding me of our predicament.

"Can you release us? My friend needs medical attention. If we get out now, maybe I can treat him with the supplies at camp or get him to help."

She shook her head sadly.

"Even if we open the doors now, your friend cannot survive. His wound is mortal, I'm afraid."

She looked back toward the sarcophagus, tilting her head slightly as if listening to a voice, then nodded.

"The master wishes to speak to you. You must release him, as only a mortal can do so."

After everything we had been through on this expedition, I feared a deception of some sort. Still, we were clearly at the mercy of this woman or whatever else was holding us here. I looked at Douglas, who raised his eyebrows as if to say we had nothing to lose at this point.

I walked to the glowing golden sarcophagus, which was about 8 feet tall, in the shape of a man. I examined it, looking for some way to open the case. I ran my hands along both sides, but it seemed to be solid and unbroken by any seams, latches or handles.

"You must use the Eye of Kentenkamen," our guide offered.

"The Eye?"

"In your pocket."

I reached into my right pocket and pulled out the chunk of stone that had been mixed with the sapphire-like stones in the previous chamber. As I held it in my hand, it started to quickly warm, becoming so hot that I dropped it. It fell to the stone floor, shattering as it landed to reveal a glowing red orb about the size of an eyeball.

I picked up the orb, no longer hot to the touch. On the sarcophagus, the right eye of the golden face glowed. A corresponding indentation on the left side was the right size for the one in my hand. I placed it on the sarcophagus, which began to vibrate. The eyes grew brighter, then the sarcophagus split down the middle, opening to reveal a mummy, preserved in spotless white linen. The inner walls of the sarcophagus appeared to be the source of light that had brightened the room.

As I pondered what to do next, the light, already unbelievably bright, grew stronger. I backed a few feet away, fearing what would happen next. An incredible explosion of light left me temporarily blinded. When my vision cleared, I found a tall man standing in front of me, garbed in brown ceremonial robes, as if preparing to offer a religious ritual. Standing six and half feet tall, with dark hair and olive features, he cast a powerful presence.

"I have waited many years to meet you," he intoned. "Have watched you, observed you. Both of you," he said nodding toward Douglas.

"I can't say I'm happy to make your acquaintance," I responded angrily. "I've played your game. Now release us!"

"No, we have much to discuss, but first," he paused, pointing with his left hand at Douglas, who exclaimed in pain. I attempted to stop him, but was frozen in place with a gesture of his right hand. After less than a minute, Kentenkamen lowered both hands. Douglas slipped into a faint and I ran to him. To my astonishment, while the blood remained on his shirt, the wound was completely healed.

"How did you ... Thank you," I said. "Now, will you please release us."

"I am afraid it is not a perfect fix," he said. "That power is limited to this temple. If he leaves the area of the temple, the wound will prove fatal. It is the same reason that we could close the chamber to protect the two of you. It is also how we were able to release our guardians to eliminate Bradley, but could not stop him from infiltrating your expedition."

"What are we supposed to do for Douglas, then?" I asked, ignoring the comment about "eliminating" Bradley for now.

"This infiltration shows that we must be better prepared. That man Bradley got dangerously close to destroying everything. Luckily, he led no one else here, but I fear it is only a matter of time. Your friend will be able to live as long as he stays here and helps guard against future attacks."

"So he helps you or he dies? He's essentially your prisoner!"

"He has free will," Kentenkamen responded. "Without my interference, he would have died. This is the only way."

"I can't believe that."

"It's fine, Blake." I realized with a start that Douglas had regained consciousness. "Trust me. While I was unconscious, I saw … everything. This is important. You know I've been at loose ends since the war. This is a chance to do something that matters to the world."

I was at a loss for words, but looking at his face, I could see a contentment and sense of satisfaction I had not seen from my friend since the war.

"As I said, we have much to discuss," Kentenkamen said. "We see the future, but it is not always clearly defined. There are also those working against us who wish to change the course of history to their own ends.

"We cannot preserve the right path on our own. That means we had to rely on outsiders to help. When necessary we have warned of disasters. Some we have prevented, some we have not.

"We have decided it is now time to take a more active role. *You* are part of that solution."

"And how is that?"

"We need warriors for right. There is a great evil coming to the world. It is unclear … but we can see chaos, destruction that dwarfs that seen during the last war. Without preparation, we fear that evil will triumph. It is many years away, but the forces of good must be ready. The margin for error is miniscule."

I had figured out where he was going with this idea. "What do you expect me to do? I'm just one man!"

"You will not be alone. You are the first, but we are preparing for this fight. It is time for us to act.

"I will not lie to you. This will not be easy. You will have great power, but also great responsibility. You will be blessed and you will be cursed. You will have great power and strength. You will not be immortal, but like my other followers you will age much slower than any mortal. That means you will see the people you love age and fade away while you will be little changed."

My mind was reeling. Douglas was now standing next to me and I looked to my friend again. He gripped my shoulders, looked into my eyes with a steely confidence.

"Blake, you are my brother in arms. Remember the oath we took in France? This is the moment."

I drew myself to my full height, and turned back to face Kentenkamen.

"And what do you expect me to do for these 'many years' before this evil comes, then?"

Kentenkamen smiled, recognizing the acceptance in that statement.

"To keep doing what you've been doing all your life. Fight for what is right, defend the weak. You will return to your home and use your new-found abilities to combat evil there. When the time comes to join the fight, you will know."

As he finished speaking, Kentenkamen stretched both arms toward me, palms out. There was a flash of light, then nothing …

My vision cleared and I found myself still standing in the same spot. Douglas remained next to me, but there was no sign of Kentenkamen or his disciple. The room was once again dark, with the exception of our lone flashlight. The sarcophagus was closed and I briefly wondered if the entire conversation had been a hallucination brought on by the blow to my head. Douglas was still healed, however, and imbued with the same confident attitude.

I heard the stone sliding open behind us, letting light enter the room from the bulbs we had set up out there what seemed a decade ago. Douglas and I both stepped carefully through the opening, not sure what to expect on the other side.

"I think I'm going to have some cleaning up to do," Douglas muttered.

The room was strewn with debris. Anything loose in the space had been thrown about as if by a great storm. Behind a large overturned stone bench, we discovered Bradley, head cleanly separated from his body as if with one swipe.

"Blake ..." Douglas whispered, pointing at the large jackal soldier statue in the northeast corner. The soldier appeared unchanged, with the exception of the blood staining the large scythe in his hands.

October 7, 1922
Entry in Journal of Blake Randolph

Writing this as we depart Alexandria on the H.M.S. Clason for the journey back to New York City.

It seems rather pointless to continue this journal, as I don't expect anyone will ever read it now. What really happened there must be guarded with my life. Still, it is helpful to get my thoughts down on paper.

It took several days, but the authorities there have allowed me to leave. I have begun my journey back home.

The story Douglas and I agreed on was that the expedition was waylaid by bandits before we ever made any discoveries. We knew that keeping the secret of Kentenkamen was paramount. I'm not sure the Egyptian authorities believed me, but we arranged the evidence to be quite convincing.

It helped that we have Gamal playing the villain in this version, setting us up for their attack, selling us out for the money. It seems his reputation precedes him. I brought most of the bodies and one truck, heavily damaged, back with me. Douglas helped prepare the truck and simulate the damage from the attack. I left Gamal at the temple, explaining that he and his band of brigands took off with the other truck.

When we had completed our work, Douglas and I returned to the entrance of the temple.

"We've certainly gotten ourselves into something this time," I said. "You be careful out here."

"You be careful out *there*," he replied, offering his hand. "I think we're both going to need some luck."

"Godspeed, Douglas."

"Godspeed, Blake."

With that, he turned and walked back into the temple of Kentenkamen. I made my way to the truck to begin the long journey back to Alexandria. Strangely, I had no doubt I would find my way back without a guide.

As I reached the truck, a great gust of wind came up, blowing sand in every direction. I ducked into the cab, waiting for it to clear. When the wind finally died down, I could see that all evidence of the temple, the dig and our campsite had been buried under a thick layer of desert.

Epilogue
October 22, 1922

It was nearly 11 a.m. when the sun shining through the east window finally hit Blake Randolph's face, awakening him.

After delays enroute, and dealing with more officials in New York, he had finally arrived at St. Paul's Union Depot the previous evening. The entire ordeal had left him exhausted. So exhausted that all he had done last light was collapse in bed, not even bothering to unpack his trunk. *Or hide his journal*, he thought with a start, suddenly sitting up.

As he sprang from his bed, Blake heard the crash of his trunk slamming shut and turned to see David holding the journal.

"I … I … is this true?" his 13-year-old brother asked.

"How much did you read?"

"All of it! What *happened* out there?"

It seemed as if a million thoughts ran through Blake's mind in the next few seconds. Then, he smiled, nodding to himself.

"Sit down, David. I've got a story to tell you."

A Tip of the Cowl

The origin story of the Red Jackal wasn't clear when I first created the character. I had a vague notion that it would have something to do with Egypt (hence the name), but beyond that … to be determined.

The inspiration for this idea came about after I read a report in 2016 that scientists had determined that a dagger found in King Tut's tomb was of "extraterrestrial origin." While the headline had me thinking of stargates and aliens building the pyramids, it actually was that the metal used in this dagger had been determined by scientists to have come from a meteorite.

While the dagger didn't make it into this story (we'll see down the road), the idea of a supernatural power or one not of this world stuck with me. Combine that with the classic Universal mummy pictures, and Kentenkamen was born.

When I sat down to write this story, it was originally going to just be notes for me – the bible of the character, as it were. I ended up having so much fun with it that I fleshed it out to tell the full tale of the birth of the Red Jackal. Plus, it gave me a chance to share how the Jackal's 13-year-old brother stumbled on the truth!

A note on some of the technology used in the story. The cameras referred to are based on real-life inventions of that era. The Aeroscope was built by Polish inventor Kazimierz Proszynski in England shortly before World War I. The cameras were used by the British War Office to record battle footage during the war. They were known as the "camera of death" because so many of the combat cameramen were killed while using them.

As for the Fowlercam, it never existed, but the idea is based on early prototypes produced by American Lee de Forest and German inventors Josef Engl, Joseph Massolie and Hans Vogt.

About the Author

Jonathan W. Sweet is an award-winning journalist and the author of nine books. He has also contributed to or edited more than 30 anthologies and collections, both fiction and non-fiction.

He is a two-time finalist for the Pulp Factory Awards, recognizing the best in modern pulp and noir genre fiction. Three of his books have been Amazon bestsellers and reviewers have called his books "essential," "invaluable" and "captivating."

He is the founder of Brick Pickle Pulp, which publishes books in the classic pulp style and the host of the *Pulp Nostalgia & Old Time Radio* and *World War II Radio* podcasts. In 2020 he was named to the "Who's Who in New Pulp."

Jonathan lives in the Twin Cities with his wife, two exceptional children and one fairly dim-witted dog.

Find more at JonathanWSweet.com.

Made in the USA
Monee, IL
23 January 2024